THE LAST VENDETTA

LEONA WHITE

Copyright © 2024 by Leona White

All rights reserved.

No part of this book may be reproduced in any form or by any electronic or mechanical means, including information storage and retrieval systems, without written permission from the author, except for the use of brief quotations in a book review.

❦ Created with Vellum

BLURB

It started with a kiss, and ended in bloodshed...

RENZO

Giulia Accardi is from a rival mafia family, which means I have to stay away at all costs.

But her beauty and innocence prevent me from staying away; I want what I can't have.

Except Giulia will never bend the knee to someone like me.

Not unless I trick her into giving me her V-card...

As soon as she's mine once, she'll be mine forever.

They say you never forget your first... Giulia sure won't, because I intend on being her last, too.

GIULIA

I kissed a man I shouldn't have at a wedding. It was wild, passionate, and sparks were flying… Until a blood-curdling scream interrupted us.

Now somebody is dead, and I'm guilty of associating with the enemy.

I know I should stay away from Renzo Bernardi, but that's easier said than done…

And after a passionate night together, there's no running away from what I've done.

Because I just gave up my cherry to a man I should hate.

And now he's not letting go.

★ *If you love age gap, enemies to lovers, dark romance & forbidden love, don't miss this new release! Read for FREE with Kindle Unlimited* ★

1

GIULIA

Giulia

Like every other party I was expected to attend, the reception for Luka Bernardi and Cecilia Romano was a bore. The same old. All the Mafia Families coming together. Mine only came to keep up appearances. These gatherings were opportunities to maintain a closer eye on enemies and friends, and those two labels interchanged often.

Everyone knew the Acardis would forever be rivals of the Bernardis. Yet, here we were, acting like we wouldn't just as easily stir up some trouble for old time's sake.

If the bride weren't a Romano, things would be tenser. As the oldest Family of this criminal world, the Romanos held the most weight, hoarded the most wealth, and flaunted the most power. The Romanos, whether we liked it or not, dictated that we try to behave tonight.

No matter how Nickolas Romano acted like an idiot right now. Surrounded by three women, all dolled up and preening for his attention while he spoke with his father, Marcus. They stood there like kings, gods among the inferior. Talking freely without a care in the world.

My lip curled in disgust at Nickolas groping one guest and pulling her closer. The girl barely hid her flinch at his rough touch.

Ugh. No thanks.

My mother would expect me to get pawed at and take it. To be submissive like a good Mafia daughter should. To roll over and let men do as they please.

"No thanks," I mumbled to myself as I walked further from the dance floor.

As the eldest daughter to my parents, Rocco and Isabella Acardi, I knew it would one day be me up there by the head table. I would be a bride, foisted into an arranged marriage. Cecilia had to go through the ordeal tonight, smiling and pretending that she was glad to be married to Luka Bernardi. That she chose it. That she welcomed a life of being his possession.

The day when it would come for me lurked closer. I was already twenty-three, and in our world, I should be snatched up soon.

All the better to pop out kids and all that drama.

I rolled my eyes, dreading my turn. There was no escaping it. I *would* be married off. Instead of wanting to complain about my circumstances, I should've spent the last hour mingling and trying to get a feel for which asshole I'd be paired up with.

My mother was strategizing. I knew she was scheming and planning here, eyeing which prospective man I could get hitched with and which Family she could benefit the most from. Everyone who mattered had shown up to be seen on Luka and Cecilia's big day. She couldn't have had a better opportunity to shop around for me than this.

But no one appealed. Not a single man stood out to me. They were all the same, ruthless, greedy, and all out for themselves.

Love wouldn't be a factor in the equation for the rest of my life. Intimacy was a joke. As I looked around at the men here, I knew arousal would be a laughing matter too.

"Giulia," my younger sister, Mariana, said as she passed me by. "You look so…"

"Oh, don't start." I smirked at her, checking that she was only getting another slice of cake to take to the table our Uncle Dario sat at. He waited, no doubt, for her to bring him that second slice she held since he wasn't able to walk well with his cane.

"If Mama saw you looking all pissy and grumpy…" Mariana teased.

"Shh," I scolded her playfully. All four of us Acardi girls were subject to our mother's constant criticism. I had it the worst, as the eldest, but I found a nugget of humor in the way Marianna could tease me about it.

"What's wrong?" she asked.

I shrugged, not bothering to invest much effort in the gesture. "Nothing, really. Just bored."

And annoyed.

Everyone here was trying to get in the Romanos' favor. And those who weren't were mooching off the chance to mingle and strike deals. No gathering was ever "fun" or "peaceful". Something was always at work. Somebody was always making plans or plotting trouble.

Knowing my mother had to be around here considering who I could marry simply upset my stomach.

It is what it is.

"Well, you're of age." Marianna smiled as she grabbed a champagne flute from the tray of a passing waiter. She thrust it to me, almost dropping

Dario's cake plate, and I hurried to help her in the fumble. "Why be bored or look so grumpy when you can just drink and make it easier?"

I took the flute, shooting her a stern look. "You mean like Father does?"

Marianna shrugged. It was her turn to suggest *it is what it is*. She had no right to push me to imbibe in alcohol. She was only fourteen, but she wasn't stupid. I bet she wished to escape this party just as much as I did, but she was limited as a minor.

Together, we glanced toward our father. He stood near our mother as she talked and talked and talked, all about being seen and heard. The glass at his lips was almost empty, and once it was, he set it down and sighed as though he immediately needed another.

"I bet it doesn't help, anyway." Marianna frowned, looking at all the guests partying here. She was the only child in attendance, and she had to feel like the odd one out. I'd argued with Mother to let Marianna stay home with Beatrice and Lucia, but she'd insisted on "checking out the options" for Mariana. If she intended to try to marry her off so soon, when she was barely an adult...

What? What can I do about it? I clenched my teeth, hating how stuck we were as Mafia daughters. I couldn't stop my sister from being paired up with someone way too old for her any more than I could tell my mother no when she matched me with some abusive jerk.

And they all were.

"Uh-oh." Marianna winced. "You look even madder now."

I smiled quickly. "I just need a breath of fresh air," I lied. Stepping outside wouldn't solve anything, but I could take a break from the cloying perfume, overwhelming cologne, and the stench of too much garlic on everyone's breath as they tried to get too close to talk and be heard over the music and chatter.

"Stay with Uncle Dario," I instructed her.

She nodded, already heading back to him at the table. "He's making it manageable."

I raised my brows. "How?"

Marianna giggled. "People watching. And making up stories ad-lib-style about them."

I smiled, heading outside with my champagne.

My mother wouldn't let me hide for long. She'd track me down and insist that I try to socialize with the men, one of whom might soon be my fiancé. Even though tonight was supposed to be all about celebrating Luka and Cecilia, all the Mafia mothers would be doing the same things my mother was doing.

Scheming. Planning. Observing. Judging.

It was all she did.

No wonder Father just steps aside and seeks the oblivion of alcohol.

I sighed, then lifted my glass to my lips.

Night had long since fallen, and out here on the smooth patio stones of the courtyard entrance, I finally welcomed a sense of peace. Of solitude. Of loneliness I wished I could count on.

How serene it would be to truly be unbothered. No sisters to help raise. No mother to appease and avoid. No leering men to dread.

Just to be.

I breathed in deeply and set my hands on the cool granite railing. My glass stood on the top of a post, shadowed by the copious flowers overflowing from the planter space. Light glittered off the rim, though, reflecting the many lights from within the ballroom I'd just left.

Music floated out, teasing my ears without the harshness of too many decibels with the conversations inside. Beyond the chords from the band, the gentle trickle of water streaming into a fountain calmed me.

This was much better. Almost Zen-like. Alone and not being criticized or considered to be anyone's pawn.

"Just for a moment," I whispered to myself. Because even if my mother didn't hurry to find me and keep tabs on me, like a freaking pet, I'd need to go back in and salvage the situation with Father. He'd drink more and more. Quicker and quicker. Loose tongues never went well, and I could always count on him to listen to me.

"Shh! Someone's going to know I'm slacking off," a woman nagged. Her tone was light and flirty, hinting at excitement.

I let my face fall into a blank stare at the navy-blue sky speckled with stars.

Someone was coming. Or a couple was.

A man's deep chuckle followed the woman's playful scolding. She giggled right after.

So much for peace.

Without turning my head, not moving from my position on this second tier of the patio, I leaned against the railing and stared at the sky. The ledge of the stone column next to me held my champagne, and the protrusion of the formation offered me a slight hiding spot.

Please, don't see me. Please, please, don't bother me. Just go away, out there, and do what you have to without making me give up this spot.

The couple didn't pause, sneaking out of the party to get into the gardens down below. They didn't spot me, but I caught enough of a glimpse as they went down the steps to the side.

Bernardi. I grimaced in annoyance.

While it would've been extremely scandalous to catch Luke Bernardi stepping away from his wedding reception to hook up with a server working at it, I wasn't even surprised to see his younger brother chasing a young woman out like this.

Renzo Bernardi was the spare brother. The second born. In other words, useless to carry on the Bernardi bloodline. He knew it too, and he exploited his freedom.

A player. A partier. A loose daredevil of a wealthy man who didn't have to work or meet his father's expectations. I imagined Giovanni Bernardi hardly cared what his second son did. And I bet Luka envied Renzo's easygoing lifestyle, sans obligations.

I was jealous myself. Being a man in our world was a blessing, autonomy and the permission to make their own choices. It sounded like a dream, and it was one this lazy punk took for granted.

He followed the server, his gaze latched on her ass as she hurried ahead of him. She held his hand, luring him out of the party area, and he tagged along behind. He wasn't grinning and excited like she was when she looked over his shoulder at him. If anything, he almost seemed bored. Like taking this employee out here for a quickie was just another thing to do. Just another way to pass the time.

His suit stretched and pulled over his muscled physique, but under the moonlight, I had plenty of illumination to really see him. Tall but not bulky. Strong but not beefy. I stared at the sexy man who was off-limits. Admitting my appreciation of Renzo Bernardi would be akin to saying I cared for the enemy. Acardis and Bernardis would never mix. That rule had been imprinted in my mind since I was young.

Still, there was no law against appreciating eye candy. I didn't see how wrong it was to simply admire a powerful, handsome man—especially in this rare moment when he wasn't aware that I spied on him.

Until he found me.

He suddenly glanced over while following the server, but the chase was over. His blue eyes lit up under the slash of light that cut through the nightscape from the many windows behind us. Lower, but not out of sight, he happened to notice me peering at him from above.

They'd reached the middle tier of the elaborate courtyard entrance, one level below me.

But his focus was no longer on the easy piece of ass he'd come out here to enjoy.

Over and over again, he glanced up at me, stuck on smirking at me for hiding away from the party.

Dammit. So much for a peaceful moment.

"Oh. You want to stop here?" The server giggled, reaching for his pants and kissing up his neck. "That's fine."

He let her reach for his buckle but stood there unimpressed with her lips on his skin.

Still, he glanced up at me with something like a naughty smile curving his mouth upward.

I rolled my eyes, irked that such an attractive man had to be such a playboy ass. Not bothering to look away, I flipped him off. *Thanks for ruining my quiet, peaceful moment.* Cut too short. As expected.

He grinned, only now reaching for the server's hands and breaking away from her. "Actually, never mind."

"What?" She pouted, lifting her hands to grab the back of his neck. "No. Come on. Right here is fine for me." Her fingers locked on his wrist as she tugged his hand to lay over her breast.

"No. No thanks." He stepped back again.

"But I—"

"No," he repeated, firmly, as he spun her around and then shoved her shoulder to get her going.

She glared at him over her shoulder. "But—"

"Get back to work," he ordered as he walked across the patio, away from her and toward the other set of stairs.

Yeah, please leave. Both of you.

I ground my teeth, watching as the girl sulked off to exit up the stairs she'd just tugged him down. At the same time, he leisurely climbed the other set.

As though he wanted to approach *me*.

I refused to turn my head. Acknowledging him would give him too much satisfaction, but with every footfall that heralded his coming closer to me in the shadows, I felt a dizzying mixture of loathing and giddiness building up inside me.

I had no reason to be excited about Renzo seeking me out. We were enemies at best. Mere acquaintances otherwise.

But there he was, leaning his forearms on the railing, mirroring my stance.

"Hiding?" he asked, his teasing tone full of amusement just to mock me.

I narrowed my eyes at the stars above, determined not to let him see how he got to me. "I *was*."

2

RENZO

Renzo

"And why would you need to hide from the fun?" I wouldn't turn and face Giulia if she was determined to resist making eye contact with me. I'd wait until she caved first. Women always did. They couldn't hold up to any kind of pressure.

"You call that fun?" She jerked her thumb over her shoulder as she straightened from the railing she'd been leaning her arms on. Although she only gave me her profile, I wasn't out of luck for a treat. Giulia Acardi, my sworn enemy, was a beautiful woman no matter how she stood, her slender curves, her long, raven hair, and those rich, dark eyes. I tried my best to avoid looking at her for too long, and only when she wouldn't notice. It felt a lot like staring into the sun.

I snorted a laugh, no longer bored since I had her company out here away from all the others. Ten minutes ago, my answer would've been simple. Fuck no. My brother's wedding was a bore, and this reception barely held my interest. I was a fan of parties. Living the easy life was more my style, but this grand ball after the ceremony was anything but fun.

Like usual, it felt like politics. Like every single person in there was the same old, operating under the same old dramatic motivations and always playing the field.

They weren't in there genuinely celebrating my brother marrying Cecilia Romano. I doubted any of them actually gave a fuck at all. All those Mafia lords and leaders were doing business as usual.

I sure as hell didn't care. I was here because I had to be, and it wasn't until that feisty, flirty server suggested I "accompany her on her break" that I woke up at the prospect of a quickie in the courtyard.

"Not really," I admitted. It wouldn't kill me to agree with her. That reception wasn't fun—not for me. "I'm just glad it wasn't me getting married today."

Luka could have all the responsibilities of giving our father a son to carry on the Bernardi name. Not me. I was spared from having to live up to any important expectations, and that was just the way I liked it.

"I bet that would crimp your style."

I smiled, still holding out to face her. She'd cave. Giulia Acardi couldn't last against me.

"And what's my 'style'?"

She splayed her hand out, gesturing to where that lusty server almost got my pants unzipped. "Screwing around. Chasing an easy lay."

I shrugged. "Not like I couldn't do that while I'm married too."

Her sigh was a long and heavy one. "True."

"Don't tell me you're one of those hopeless romantics who actually believe in monogamy."

"And don't tell me you're one of those idiotic players who actually think they can make all the women in the world come."

"I wouldn't want to make them all come."

She turned, propping her elbow on the railing to narrow her gaze at me. "Of course not. Why should a spoiled, useless man like you care about pleasing a woman?"

I pivoted, smiling easily at her haughty expression. She was just as high-maintenance as the other mistresses, wives, and daughters were inside the hall, but she still stood out, gorgeous from within with that flare of a challenge that always burned in her brown eyes.

"Do you doubt that I can make a woman happy?" I stepped closer, taunted by her carefully schooled expression. She wouldn't cower. She wouldn't retreat.

Giulia was off-limits. But knowing that didn't stop me from getting into her space and looking down at her.

I had no interest in the number of women I could fuck. It was becoming all the same thing, over and over again.

Gazing into this woman's dark eyes, I felt a flicker of something new. Something different. And something so addicting that I couldn't think of stepping back.

Our Families had never seen eye to eye, but staring into hers was like walking on a tight line of the ultimate dare.

"I doubt you would be able to discern when a woman is faking it," she quipped dryly, lowering her hooded gaze to my chest, then dragging it up to my lips. "Not that any would ever admit it."

Oh, fuck you. I grinned, turned on by her bickering and trying to belittle me.

"How about you teach me the difference?" I reached for her waist, sliding my hand along her side and reveling in her softness. Making contact was forbidden, but I didn't care. I couldn't. Surrendering to the temptation of feeling her was too good to resist.

Her breath hitched, but she kept her gaze low, locked on my lips and unwavering.

"You'd admit it."

The tip of her tongue peeked out to trace along her lips. "I would." She cleared her throat, stepping toward me until our bodies were flush. "I'd be happy to tell you how lousy you are."

You bitch. I grinned wider, wrapping my other arm around her. "Not as happy as I'd be to prove you wrong."

"As if my opinions matter?" she shot back as she laid her hand on my chest.

Beneath her fingers, my heart thumped wildly. She was forbidden. Off-limits. If my father saw me with her, he'd be peeved. If her parents noticed how close we stood, they'd flip out.

But nothing could have pulled me away. Nothing. I was riveted, locked and stuck on holding on to her and showing her a fraction of the pleasure I was capable of giving.

I pushed into her, letting her feel the bulge of my dick hardening under my pants. She did this to me. Her refusal to back down. That spirit and fire to challenge me right back. This woman turned me on like no other lover ever had. "They don't. Not at all."

She slid her hand higher, moving it over my shoulder, almost to hug me. "Then why bother proving anything—"

"Giulia?"

She tensed. Still and holding her breath, Giulia froze at the sound of her mother's voice from the doors closest to the ballroom.

I already knew she was hiding, but I didn't know how badly she wanted to keep it that way.

"Fuck." She exhaled it as she backed away. From me. From the doors. Retreating from the threat of her mother looking for her, Giulia began to escape to the next level down.

"I doubt she'd be out here," Rocco Acardi said, slurring already.

Dumb old drunk.

"Well, she has to be somewhere!" Isabella snapped. "Giulia!"

Gritting her teeth, she backed away. Slowly, quietly, and likely hoping I'd stay right where I was to block her.

Nope. Not happening. I wasn't done flirting with trouble. If Giulia was the source of it, I'd chase her right into her next hiding spot.

I followed after her, making sure to block her from her parents' view behind me. Once she realized she wasn't running off alone, she frowned, trying to turn and hurry away faster.

As we reached the stairs, her parents' voices dimmer in the distance, I caught her before she slipped and tripped on the first step down. Keeping her within my embrace, I hastened to take the stairs three at a time, almost carrying her with me.

"What—"

I didn't give her a chance to reply, tucking her against the wall on the next level down.

When I came out here, I intended to have that server suck me off on this level of the smooth stone terrace overlooking the gardens.

Now that I'd happened upon Giulia looking as bored as I'd felt, I caged her against the wall instead of that stranger.

"What…?"

Again, Giulia hissed, her sharp gaze searing me and taunting me. Her whisper should've warned me off. She spoke defensively, as hostile as ever.

But the second I slammed my lips to hers, she melted under my touch.

If she wanted to hide, I'd help. I'd tuck her into this dark corner and keep her company in the shadows.

And she was all for it. Kissing me back harder, she urged me to hold her close. Her sassy lips tasted too sweet to deny. Her tongue slipped into my mouth and slid with determination to explore. Most of all, her greedy hands latched onto me, first on the back of my head. Her nails scraped over my scalp, tingling my nerves as she held me low to her. Then as she draped her arms over my shoulders in a loose hug, she gave herself up to me.

This was wrong. It was stupid. It was impulsive, rash, and not at all planned.

But I couldn't stop. Nor could she. With her parents calling out for her on the level above us, she made out with me. While knowing she was the last woman I should ever want to fuck or hold, I devoured her and shoved my body against hers.

Hell, yes.

Now I was alive.

I wasn't bored.

She spurred me to wake up and dared me to demand more.

Most women submitted too easily, but this one... Giulia was too damn bold to resist.

"I'm telling you, she's not out here," Rocco told Isabella overhead. He sounded near tears, but I doubted it was out of sadness for not finding his daughter. That loser was always so dramatic and emotional, and his fondness for alcohol didn't help.

"Then we have to find her elsewhere," Isabella scolded.

Giulia clung to me, pulling me closer. I couldn't tell whether she was scared her parents would come down here to look for her or she was that into kissing me.

Air no longer mattered. Only the stubborn push of her lips against mine mattered. Just the weight of her body and the force of her touch mattered. Nothing else could register.

"I want to go back inside," Rocco said.

"Oh, sure, you do." Isabella's heels chased after him, but I didn't bother listening anymore.

Without her parents near, I focused on Giulia. Her soft mewls that made me harder. Those sexy moans I felt through our kiss. Every inch of her soft, petite body flush with mine.

After sucking on her tongue, I nipped her lower lip and parted for much-needed air.

"Try not to scream," I taunted as I lifted her dress up. Breathing hard, I stared at her expressive face as I reached between her legs and slipped my fingers along her wet pussy.

Dripping. Wet for me already.

I groaned, drowning with potent desire at the idea that I'd made her cream like this.

She grinned, lifting one leg to set her heel on the step closest to us. Blocked by the stairs, we were hidden in our own little bubble. It hardly mattered where we were, just so long as I could keep my hands on her.

"Scream?" she sassed back hotly, catching her breath. "Don't flatter yourself."

"You're such a hateful, spiteful bitch," I argued before I kissed her again. Only once I had her moaning against my mouth again did I push my fingers into her tight, slick heat. Leaning back to whisper against her wet, kiss-swollen lips, I dared her to argue. "You want to judge me. You want to try to piss me off by suggesting I can't please a woman?"

I pressed my two fingers in deeper, harder, and she dropped her head back against the stone wall.

"Shut up," she bickered weakly as I slid my digits deeper inside her. "Just shut up."

"You want me to stop?" I rubbed my palm over her mound, giving her clit a little rub.

She growled, gripping the back of my head and pulling me closer for a deep, brutal kiss. Her reply came in her thrusts, too, and soon, she rode my hand as I stretched her tight cunt.

"Don't make the entire night a waste of my time," she weakly answered.

I barked a single laugh. "Who invited you, anyway?"

"The bride's family," she whispered, her breaths hot against my lips.

"Sure as fuck wouldn't have been us," I promised, making sure to rub harder over her mound. "But I guess I should be grateful for this chance to take pity on you and show you how good a real man can make a woman feel."

"Do you ever shut up?" she retorted.

I lowered one arm to grab her ass. Once I had her cheek in my hand, digging my fingers into her flesh, I held her in place to piston my fingers into her harder.

She groaned, closing her eyes as she let her head fall back again, but I wasn't having it.

"Open your eyes, Giulia. Open your fucking eyes and see who's doing this to you."

Narrowing her gaze at me, she listened. She watched me, looking down to stare at my hand up her dress. She felt me, feeling my fingers pumping into her tight heat.

"You want to imply that I don't know how to handle a woman? Even someone like you?" I growled.

She whined, reaching for my head to thread her fingers through my hair. Holding me close, she sealed her mouth over mine and kissed me. Punishingly, thoroughly. I angled my head and craned my neck to meet her in the middle. Between holding her ass and fingering her cunt, I was limited in how I could hold her, but she made up for it. Securing my face to hers, she kissed me until we were both ragged for air.

"You…" She breathed faster, still humping my hand. "You shouldn't—"

"We shouldn't." I nodded as I lowered my mouth to her neck. Just below her ear, I began to trail wet, hot kisses down the delicate skin there. "We really shouldn't be doing this."

"Oh, fuck, Renzo," she groaned as I added another finger. "Oh, fuck."

I grinned, kissing down her neck and wondering how loud she'd be. Soaked and squeezing my fingers, she promised a hard orgasm. One I'd relish as a victory forever. One I'd—

A scream cut through the air.

Not hers.

She went still at the sound.

I stopped, freezing with my fingers up her cunt and my mouth open over her neck.

Another scream.

The music stopped overhead.

"What…" Giulia swallowed, shoving at me. I straightened, lifting from her neck as I pulled my fingers free. Staring at each other open-mouthed, we waited.

What the fuck was that for?

"He's dead!" My new sister-in-law's voice rang out clearly from the ballroom. Through the open doors leading into the reception, her news reached us.

"Luka!" she screamed again. "He's dead!"

I stepped back from Giulia, opening my eyes wide as I let it sink in. Panic and anger replaced lust. My heart thundered, and I struggled to breathe fast enough as adrenaline hit me hard.

My brother had been killed at his own wedding.

3

GIULIA

Giulia

Marianna stayed by my side as we entered our home. I couldn't blame her for the abrupt end of the reception an hour ago.

From the moment Cecilia screamed in the ballroom, chaos ensued. I'd never forget the terror on Renzo's face as he ran inside, and I hurried in after him to see what happened. That sight would be forever etched in my mind, too.

Giovanni Bernardi stared at his son, roaring with rage and demanding to know who'd killed him.

I'd never be able to forget that father's plea for an answer, either. So enraged and instantly shocked, he lost it. Unhinged and red-faced, he began yelling at everyone to know who'd killed Luka.

Why?

How?

But most of all, he repeated his desperate demands to know who'd murdered the groom.

Any parent would be shocked and furious. Hurt and lost. Bewildered and aggrieved. No one ever wanted to see their own child to the grave. I often felt like a parent myself, raising my younger sisters, and I couldn't comprehend that heart-deep loss.

My father's reactions, however, made no sense.

He'd been moody and sad all evening, acting like his usual depressed self, but the moment Cecilia screamed that her husband was dead, the Romano guards closest to the head table had attacked *him*. Rocco Acardi had no reason to be struck, but in the heat of the moment, he had been beaten badly, caught in the commotion that followed Cecilia's screams as Luke lay dead, slumped over the pristine-white fabric of the head table he'd shared with his wife.

"Is Father going to be okay?" Marianna glanced at the Acardi men helping him inside our mansion. He plopped onto the couch, breathing hard with blood streaming down his face. Our father wasn't the fittest man, but he looked every bit of his age, worn and bruised as he groaned and sank into the cushions.

He didn't look good, and I couldn't fault her for being startled, but he would live. Violence was a given in this life—but not like this. Not every wedding ended with murder. Not all outings resulted with our father being struck directly like this.

"Of course. Of course," I replied.

Mother continued to rage at him, demanding to know why he hadn't defended himself. Why he'd let those Romano guards strike out at him.

She didn't care that he was hurt, only that he'd let the Acardi name look weak when he didn't act like a strong, fit man half his age and defend himself even though he was outnumbered.

She didn't care about Marianna being traumatized and witnessing such an uproar of violence at the wedding. My sister was only fourteen, too young to be thrust into this much violence. But she didn't care.

Nor would she care about Lucia and Beatrice hearing the noise and coming downstairs, scared and alarmed by the shouting.

Mother didn't notice or pause in her rants at my father, too used to my acting like a mother in her place.

"Go on upstairs. Back to bed." I shooed them away, trying to block the sight of the blood on our father's face. Lucia saw anyway and frowned, but she wrapped her arm around Beatrice's shoulders and guided her to turn around.

"Take them back to bed," I told Marianna. "They're too young to be worried about this."

You are too, I thought.

She listened, leading our younger sisters back up the stairs. Father was wounded, but it wasn't like he was dying. Still, this was a startling sight. If any violence visited us, it was when one of our soldiers was hit or killed. Father seldom did anything on the "front line" of any meeting, and a wedding wasn't a scene of war.

Or it shouldn't have been.

Luka Bernardi's death would rock our world. Everyone would be impacted in some way, whether as a reminder of our mortality, an example of how deep rivalries and hatred could run, or another demonstration that we surrounded ourselves with violent people.

It still felt surreal, and part of my stubbornness to let Luka's death sink in was because of where I was and what I was doing when the news broke out.

I'd been hiding from my parents, sheltered by Renzo while he—

Stop. I had no business wanting him to touch me like that. I had even less business demanding that he kiss me more. And it was not the time to think about it at all. His brother had been killed. My father was wounded.

Not the time to be thinking about what I'd been pulled from.

I exhaled as my sisters trudged up the stairs, glancing back at me, then at Father on the couch.

"You too," Uncle Dario said. He approached me slowly, wincing and leaning heavier on his cane. "Help your sisters."

I shot him a look and shook my head. "No." I'd be damned if I was shoved aside too. News of Luka being killed at his wedding was nothing to sweep under the rug. I had to know what had happened to Renzo's brother. Staying up-to-date about others was a necessity, but I *had* to know now.

"What were you thinking?" Mother demanded, screeching at Father. "Why on earth would you intervene?"

"I was there," he replied shakily, wincing as a soldier applied a compress to the cut on his brow. "I was there, by that table, and I thought it would make sense to help or defend or…"

Dario approached them with me, furrowing his brow. "Defend? *You?*"

Father scowled at him. "What does that mean?"

Uncle Dario didn't react to his angry expression. "You aren't any defender."

"Oh, no more than *you* are?" Father snapped.

I held on to Dario's upper arm, showing my support at that jab. Father was hurting, but he had no right to attack like that.

It was too cruel of a dig at his younger brother. Dario had been handicapped years ago in a turf battle war. Disabled, unable to use his leg well, and rendered infertile, Dario was half the man he once was—physically.

"You are a leader. Head of the Acardi Family," Dario reminded him. "If anyone needed defense, it shouldn't have been you to personally provide it."

"Why them?" Mother demanded. She seethed, pacing and absolutely livid. Her face didn't show it. She'd had far too much surgery to truly reveal any emotion, but I heard it in her snarl.

"The Romanos would have appreciated the help," Father replied feebly, shifting to sit more comfortably.

"The Romanos?" she screamed, incredulous. "Cecilia Romano wasn't killed. Luka Bernardi was! And Marcus Romano will be out for blood. He'll take this as a personal insult. And you had to butt in and get in the way. Now he'll be looking at *you* as a complication in all of—"

"Enough." I stepped closer to stand in the way of Mother's pacing.

"Don't you dare tell me *enough*," she sneered at me. "Marcus Romano is not someone we want to have as an enemy."

I narrowed my eyes at her, trying to understand. "But you're fine with Luka being killed, right? Because he's a Bernardi?"

"Shut up, you fool. You don't know what you're talking about." She shoved to get around me to yell in Father's face again.

This was far from the first time she'd talked to me like that. It wasn't the first time she'd talked to him like that, either. This was just the vile sort of woman she was.

"She's right," Father said, surprising me with that defense. "You won't care that a Bernardi was killed."

"You only care about the Acardi name," I reminded her.

"As I should," she yelled. "Giovanni's going to be furious and out for blood too, and I can't worry about that."

"He already was," Dario said as he lowered to a chair, wincing with the descent.

He was. Renzo's father was fighting his guards who kept him back from everyone else. Other Bernardi soldiers took over, defending both Renzo and Giovanni, worried that another hit would come.

None did. In fact, Luka hadn't been *hit* either.

It wasn't a gunshot wound that ended Luka's life, but a poison. Nothing showed on Luka outwardly, but the medic of the Bernardi guard staff quickly concluded that he'd been poisoned. The details were fuzzy. Everything seemed so sudden and impossible, which made it difficult to accept and understand, but I did hear the whispers through the guests that they'd deduced it to be a poisoning.

"You fucking idiot," Mother continued to rant. "You had to rush close and risk the Romanos thinking *you* were killing someone up there."

"Cecilia screamed and it caused everyone to react," he argued weakly. Staring ahead, he zoned out and seemed like he was stuck in a shell, looking out from the inside and lacking control to do anything but press that cloth to his wound.

"No one else was harmed," Dario added, as though that could appease Mother as she paced and ranted like a caged bull ready to charge at anything that she could identify as a target or irritant. She always prioritized her image, *our* image, and she valued the Acardi name and standing above all else. "Once Marcus settles down, once Cecilia is comforted for this loss," he said as slowly and evenly as he likely could, "I'm sure that no Romano will target Rocco for being there."

"In the heat of the moment," I added, "the Romano guards likely attacked any and everyone near Cecilia when she screamed." I hadn't been there to witness it all. By the time I'd run after Renzo into the ballroom, Father was already being pulled back by Acardi guards.

All three Families had split. While Giovanni mourned Luka and demanded answers from the startled wedding guests, we'd all been wise to part in the huge venue space. Wars had broken out over less than a murder or assassination, and accusations would no doubt come flinging from everywhere. I had to agree with my uncle, though. In the spur of the moment, yes, Marcus Romano and his guards were right to be suspicious of my father being near the murdered groom. Once things calmed down, he would probably want to know who'd killed his son-in-law and seek revenge.

"They'll question everyone," Dario continued calmly. "The guards were everywhere. Cameras, too. People will talk. This will settle one day, and this matter of striking out at Rocco will be old news."

Mother huffed, shaking her head as she resumed pacing. As she whirled around quickly, she locked her glare on me.

"Where were *you* when this happened?" she demanded. I heard every note of disdain in her ugly tone. She loathed having to ask me about where I was when Luka was killed, like I shouldn't ever dare to set a foot outside the boundaries of her expectations for me. Like a chained pet, a thing to be placed and ordered about.

She stalked back to me, and I refused to cave at all. I remained perfectly still, not betraying a single hint of emotions as she got in my face.

"Where were you, Giulia?" She pointed her finger at my face.

"Your father and I had just come in from searching for you when this all happened. Where were you?"

I blinked, shaking my head slightly as though suggesting she was being ridiculous to snap at me like this. "Me? Why does it matter where I was?"

Her upper lip curled. She slitted her eyes and tried to force such a stiff expression of loathing that she resembled a frigid dragon about to roar at me.

Talking back was *not* permitted in this house. Before she could slap me or try to punish me, though, I kept going.

"Are you trying to imply that *my* whereabouts matter? That *I* could have anything to do with Luka's death?" She couldn't sound any more ridiculous.

"Where were you?" She wouldn't let up, ignoring anything I replied with. "Huh? Where the hell were you hiding?"

I didn't bother to say that I wasn't hiding. I was and we both knew it. This wasn't the first wedding or Family gathering I'd tried to sneak away from and have a moment of peace. At home, she was constantly nagging me and on my ass. She harassed me or my sisters. Or my father. All of us. She spared no one her judgment and criticism.

I couldn't tell her. I would never. She could put me on the spot as much as she wanted, and I would never tell her where I was.

"Who were you talking to?" she shouted, growing more frustrated when I stared her down.

I'll never say. I wasn't that stupid.

Remaining a virgin was expected. I had to stay clean, untouched for whatever marriage she would arrange for me. My own body wasn't mine to do with as I pleased, and already, I broke that rule so much. When Renzo helped me hide from my parents on the patio, he showed me so much pleasure—or got me so damn close to it. I hadn't been able to come. He'd pushed me close, fingering me like that, but Cecilia's screams had cut it too short.

No way could I ever tell her the truth. He hadn't fucked me. I remained intact. It wasn't as though he'd penetrated me to change my true virginal status. My pussy throbbed as I thought back to the thrill of his touch there, deeper than my own fingers could ever explore, but with far more force, and somehow, more skill.

In that one-time, unexpected meeting, he showed me that he knew how to master my body much more than I ever could.

"Giulia!" I almost flinched at her shout, lost to the thoughts of Renzo.

He'd be suffering. His anger about Luka's death wouldn't fade anytime soon. It almost felt wrong to lust for him, but with how we'd been interrupted, I couldn't help it. I was lingering, unfinished, and it aggravated me to no end.

"Where were you when Luka was killed?" she demanded.

Others would ask. Everyone would want to know who was where and what happened when. The law enforcement wouldn't be contacted. We were all our own judges and executioners. But I had to be prepared.

My mother could demand answers until she turned blue in the face. I didn't care. If anyone else asked…

I held my breath, stunned and anxious about what Renzo would say when he might be asked the same questions as everyone tried to piece together who was where up until the minute Cecilia realized that Luka was dead.

I have to get ahold of him. Renzo and I had to talk. If I could get word to him, I could beg him to lie. He couldn't be spreading around that he was with me. That I could back up his alibi.

Reaching out to him wouldn't be easy. Not in the aftermath of his brother's death. It was no minor matter.

I have to.

And as soon as I spoke to him to clarify that we had to have our lies in sync, I'd need to forget all about that torrid moment we'd shared. It was cut far too short. It had happened so suddenly, out of nowhere, but that was all we could ever have.

I knew it.

But I loathed that a private moment with him could never happen again.

4

RENZO

Renzo

The ballroom was still crowded when I insisted on taking my father home. Many soldiers remained, both to clean up the scene and to begin handling the investigation. Multiple leaders within the Bernardi Family would supervise. Among them, answers would be collected. No stone would remain unturned.

One way, sooner or later, we would know who'd dared to kill Luka tonight. At his own fucking wedding.

As I escorted my father to the large mansion he called home, I let all the emotions run through me. Anger. Worry. Anxiety. Hatred.

Sadness, too, but it wasn't as deep of a feeling. Luka and I were never close. Two years separated us, but it could have very well been twenty years.

Since birth, we were treated differently. He was the eldest. He'd carry on the family name. Everything fell on his shoulders, not mine, and as such, we weren't raised the same. We weren't expected to grow up as brothers, as siblings. With his status as the heir, he had to be taught from the beginning how to behave, and his upbringing made him an asshole.

I didn't want to speak ill of the dead—even the newly dead—but there was no love lost between us.

Still, it was a loss. His death was a shocking crime, and it would hit us hard.

I glanced again at my father as I parked. Drivers stood at the ready, but I told them all to leave us. I'd wondered if he'd speak on the ride home, but no matter how many times I checked in the rear mirror, he remained still and zoned out in the backseat.

Once we arrived home, he moved with more effort. He still seemed to be in a trance, not completely with it and alert after seeing his first-born dead.

"Gio," I said, calling him as he preferred, always by his first name.

He held up his hand as he stalked toward his study, warding me from speaking.

I knew better than to leave his side. Without anything being said, he expected me to follow him. After such a night, I didn't want to have him face this loss alone. It was just the two of us now, and we would stick together.

But I had nothing to offer him. Luka was his son. I was his spare.

Or I had been until tonight.

Gio and I were never close, and it showed in how stilted we were in his study.

I didn't know what to say. I hardly knew what to think.

Did he want comfort? I doubted it. Was he waiting on me to take action? I never had before.

All I could do was struggle with every sentiment that hit me.

I was furious that someone had dared to kill a Bernardi groom at his wedding.

I was worried that Gio would expect me to step up in my brother's place.

And I was impatient. I had to figure out where to hit, how to strike back. Luka and I were never close. We weren't traditionally sentimental as brothers, but he was one of my family members. I would avenge him. No matter what.

"It's on you now," he stated gruffly as he reclined into his leather chair near the fireplace. No flames roared there, not in the summer heat we suffered now. Regardless, it was his place. His throne, I used to think when I was younger. The place where he'd sat on countless occasions to order Luka around.

Now it was my turn.

My turn that I thought I'd never have. Never wanted.

"You are my son, Renzo."

I remained locked in place, biting my cheek. He didn't add *now*. I was his son *now*, and he'd treat me as the next in line.

"You will need to step up and take the responsibility that Luka always had."

I exhaled, trying to keep my breath steady. "He's only been dead for a couple of hours."

He slammed his hand on the side table, causing the lamp on it to rattle. "Are you shirking from what's expected of you? Already?"

I heaved out a deep breath. "No. I won't. I'm not."

"I expect you to find your brother's killer." He slammed his lips in a thin line.

"Of course."

"And kill them," he growled.

"I know." I didn't roll my eyes. I wasn't that stupid, but the sooner he stopped treating me like a moron, the faster we could make progress in here.

I didn't bother worrying about his reactions. I didn't waste another second thinking about his mental health or how he was taking this. Giovanni Bernardi was a leader. He was the Boss of the Family, and of course, he would want to move straight into action. This was how he retaliated. With action. With swift decisions. Not with tears. If he had the ability to express any other emotions than anger or authority, I wouldn't know. He never showed it in public, or in front of me.

"So far, all the soldiers closest to Luka are providing incomplete and sketchy reports."

He waved his hand, dismissing me indifferently. "Of course. It's only just happened," he growled. Although he did raise his brows, almost surprised that I'd been paying attention all the while after Luka was announced dead. He probably assumed I never noticed anything, too busy partying and living my life, but I was always aware. Even if I was the spare, I was a Bernardi, and our enemies weren't kind.

"But I can't see how it wouldn't be Rocco Acardi," I added.

Thinking of that old drunk peeved me because the first thought of him pushed me into recalling his daughter. Giulia felt so sweet under my lips, her cunt wrapped around my fingers. I would've stayed just like that, pleasuring and teasing her until I'd prove her sassy mouth wrong. That I wasn't some lackluster lover.

"Don't be rash." He sat up, sighing. "Reports will take time. You cannot rush to conclusions and kill anyone and everyone who comes to mind."

Again, I withheld from groaning at his patronizing tone. *I fucking know that.*

"He was right there. He was up there near them at the head table when he was found dead," I reminded him. I doubted he'd forgotten. He'd been in the room when it happened, and I'd rushed in there from the patio.

The Romano guards hurried close to secure the situation, and in doing so, they'd attacked Rocco. It didn't look good, but I was coming in blind. I had to get more answers before acting on anything.

"If I had to point fingers," he said, narrowing his eyes and staring at the fireplace, "I'd be looking at the Romanos."

"Nickolas or Marcus?" I asked of the son and father.

"Either." Gio scowled. "Both of them voiced concerns about Luka before the marriage. Nickolas disliked him ever since that one whore died."

I knew exactly what he was speaking about. I couldn't remember her name, but both Luka and Nickolas favored her. She'd died under suspicious circumstances, and Nickolas accused Luka of having a hand in her death since it happened at a Bernardi residence.

"Marcus may be wealthy," he said, "but he's an unscrupulous bastard I'll never fully trust."

But you trusted him enough to let your son marry his daughter?

For so long, I'd turned my eye and ignored all the layers of complicated Mafia laws and grudges. It never mattered before, and I hated that it would have to be my world now.

We argued back and forth for a bit about our suspicions, and he told me more about which of the men would answer to me now.

In the end, I was too impatient to sit around and wait, too restless to talk and speculate. Things like this would take time, but I didn't want to be idle.

Rocco Acardi had behaved suspiciously, and I wanted to jump on the action now. If he'd killed my brother, he would be home and feeling guilty. Acting out of sorts. Vulnerable, even with that remorse. Or maybe stupidly high on the victory of killing a Bernardi.

"I will avenge him," I vowed sincerely before I took my leave.

I set out to begin that process now. If Rocco wasn't guilty, then I'd need to dig deeper and figure out who was. Grieving and mourning wouldn't happen now. Action was necessary. I had to show my father that I would step up, even at these hardest moments.

And that was why I arrived at the Acardi residence late into the night. After parking a ways back to avoid being detected by their patrolling guards, undoubtedly on high alert with their boss attacked at the wedding, I snuck closer and closer.

Gio was wrong to assume I didn't know anything about what it took to be a ruthless Mafia man. I'd always been loyal to the Family, even if I never had to do much. Stealth came easily to me, but I'd fine-tuned that skill set by sneaking around with women. Getting into married women's beds or running out of coveted mistresses' homes, I'd learned how to get around without being detected, and that was precisely what I did at the Acardi residence.

Getting up close to the back entrance wasn't difficult, but I waited outside for a long while to better gauge when I could pop in and find Rocco. Patience was the key to any secretive mission. The longer I stalled just outside the doors, the better I could track the guards' movements and predict when the way would be clear.

Once I snuck in, I hustled through the hallways and stuck to the shadows, seeking out the master suite where Rocco would no doubt be resting or preparing to retire.

Maybe it's too late. He had taken a beating from the Romano guards at the wedding. Rocco Acardi wasn't fit. He wasn't that old, either, but he seemed to be one of those leaders who relied too heavily on his men to do all the dirty work. Gio still worked out, but his health complications seemed to linger and matter more than they used to.

I found Rocco too soon. Upstairs, in a lounge room, he was passed out on a couch. No guards stood outside the doors of the drunk man snoring away. Blood had been cleared from his brow. A fat bandage covered the cut. It had to be the half-empty bottle of wine still clutched in his hand that had helped knock him out.

I hesitated, wondering whether I should kill him right here and now.

I could, but the question remained. *Should I?* He was asleep, vulnerable and out of it. I could walk up and slice his neck. The end.

No. I couldn't. Not like this. I had to be able to prove to Gio that I could step up and take over the responsibilities now thrust upon my shoulders. Killing Rocco without the proof that he'd murdered Luka wouldn't do me any good.

If he was the one to poison my brother, only he could confess to the act.

Waking him up would be the best course of action. As I stepped out to do just that, to rouse him and demand answers, guards walked outside. I knew the sound of their steps already. Thudding and heavy. Booted, heavy men. But a woman's voice went with them.

"I want patrols increased overnight," Isabella Acardi ordered. "That worthless drunk of mine won't think to tell you, but I insist on it. On his behalf."

"Yes, ma'am."

I stayed plastered to the wall until it seemed that they'd gone by. While the risk of more guards would make it trickier to get out, I wasn't worried. Not yet.

The sound of a door opening at the other end of this suite peeved me. Isabella was likely over there, and if the sound of light footsteps nearing this more open lounge area where Rocco slept were hers, she'd find me in seconds.

Fuck. Dealing with that vapid old woman wasn't high on my list of things to do. Ever. Rocco was a drunk idiot, but his wife was nasty, cruel and always judgmental, wanting to impress everyone but quick to demand respect she didn't deserve.

I turned out of the room, escaping into the hall. Before she could find her sleeping husband—or me, spying—I jogged down the long corridor and thought on the fly. I'd need to reroute my escape, but I wasn't nervous. Adjustments could always be made. I was nimble on my feet, fast and quick-thinking.

Until I opened a pair of doors at the end of the hall, double doors that I could have sworn would lead to a stairwell past an upstairs ballroom. At least that was what I expected from the shape of that side of the mansion.

It wasn't.

I'd crossed the threshold into a private wing.

Giulia's wing.

I closed the door behind me, quietly, and still, she was oblivious to the fact that she had a visitor. My arrival made me more of something like a trespasser, but I'd timed it to the best moment possible.

She stood in the middle of her bedroom, pulling her dress off. Smooth, tan skin flexed as she twisted to remove the garment I'd shoved up on the rear patio at the wedding. I'd thrust my fingers under that thin layer of black lace. My hand had gripped that lush ass cheek, revealed with the high arch of her thong.

As she turned, tossing the dress to a cushioned bench positioned before a vanity, she met my gaze.

Fuck me.

I still hadn't recovered from how we'd been ripped from the hot moment we shared at the wedding.

My lips tingled with a phantom touch from her alluring, sharp-witted mouth. I recalled with clarity how tightly she'd clenched around my fingers, pulsing and throbbing, slick with her juices as I played with her.

And I wanted her all over again.

"Renzo?"

Her voice was just a whisper, one full of surprise and desire. As she lowered her gaze to my crotch, I knew she'd noticed how instantly I was aroused again. The thought of her was enough to make me think of enjoying her submission again. Seeing her forced me to be close to tenting up my pants.

She kept her arms down, not shying away or rushing to cover herself up. Those huge tits stood high and full, taunting me as she stood tall in nothing but a lacy bra and thong. Her legs remained in place, not carrying her to hide at my catching her undressing.

With lust burning in her eyes, no doubt reflecting the way I stared at her, she licked her lips and watched me approach.

"Renzo, what are you doing here?" At the sound of a quick gasp behind her, she spun, finding her sister waking up on a chaise near the window.

Goddammit! I dropped to the carpet, rolling toward the bed to hide as the scared girl who'd been sleeping out of my sight in the room woke up fully and drew in a breath to scream.

5

GIULIA

Giulia

Renzo!

I turned, grabbing my robe that was resting on the foot of my bed.

What is he doing here?

I'd have to wait to ask. He was quick to drop and hide at the sound of Beatrice waking up. Facing her now, I hurried to comfort her.

After I left my parents down the hall, I came to my room and found my youngest sister curled up on the chaise where she liked to read. Just to be near me, she always said. With the fright from earlier, I wasn't surprised that she came into my room wanting some sense of security. It was the middle of the night, though, and she hadn't lasted long with her e-reader. It lay on her lap as she sat up, happening to wake right when freaking Renzo entered my room.

"Shh." I rushed to calm her, reaching out to her and hugging her.

I didn't need her screaming in fright, scared by the sight of a man in my room.

"I saw—"

I held her close, urging her to stand. "A dream," I cooed. "It was just a dream."

She nodded, furrowing her brow as I led her away from the chaise. Making sure to block any view of Renzo on the floor, I held my robe out and hustled her to the door. "You'll feel better in your own bed, not that little chaise."

"I know," she admitted before she yawned, blinking with her eyes still half sleepy. "I just wanted to wait up for you to come in your room. I don't like it when they fight."

Neither do I. I walked her to the door and kissed her brow as I opened it.

For all I knew, Renzo could be gone again by the time I returned from seeing Beatrice back in her own bed. I kissed her brow, eager to go back and see why the hell that man had snuck into our house, let alone into my room.

His brother had only been dead for mere hours. So, as I walked back to my room, opened the door, then closed it behind me, I wondered *why*. Was he here to seek comfort? Was he eager to finish what we started and couldn't finish, resorting to intimacy to avoid reacting to his brother's death?

"Renzo?" I whispered as I crept over the carpet, my bare feet silent.

Was it all my imagination? No. Beatrice saw him too. I felt every—

He stepped out from around my dresser, stalking toward me. At once, I revisited that instant connection and flare of heat that his heated stare incited in me. Feeling his gaze rove over me lit me up inside, fraying my nerves into a mess. I hadn't dreamed this up. This was twice now that I was suffering from the tension and awareness of his smoldering stare.

"Renzo," I repeated, scolding him the best I could in these conditions. Like being nearly naked. And us alone. In my room. That he was even here.

"What are you doing here?" I wrapped my robe over myself, vainly trying to cover up and at least look like I was attempting to be modest. Alarm registered in my mind, dulling the immediate arousal he'd stoked by looking at me like that.

"Fuck, Giulia," he rasped, reaching me and trying to grab my waist.

I sidestepped his hands, glaring at him the best I could while resisting my desire to lunge at him and pick up where we'd left off.

He wasn't some new, shiny thing. We'd known each other since we were children, always near but never friends. The longstanding antagonism between our Families prevented us from ever becoming more than mutually loathed acquaintances, but we'd always been aware of the other lurking in the background.

Only now, since he'd found me wanting a moment of peace while I hid at that party, did I feel this sweeping, all-consuming need to be near him.

To feel him.

And kiss him until he growled and clutched at me tighter.

He was just as conflicted as I was. His gaze turned hotter, and his face went taut with more grooves on his brow. Scowling and narrowing his eyes, he silently warned me not to shy away or fight back again.

Too bad.

"Why are you here?" I asked again, crossing my arms to hold my robe together.

"I came to see your father," he said, setting his hand on my waist.

His touch burned me. This thin robe did nothing as a proper layer of protection. I didn't dodge away, too thrilled with the unique excitement from having his fingers on me again.

"In *my* room?" I challenged, refusing to show him how much his rough hold got to me. I shivered, hating my body's reaction, and he placed his other hand on my back. Within his embrace, I was trapped. Under his hot gaze and caught between his big hands, he had me right where he wanted me, looking like he was eager to resume where we'd left off.

"I saw him drunk and asleep at the other end of the hall," he explained, stepping closer as he breathed quicker. Tension built between us, hot and sizzling as we stared each other down. His hands didn't leave me, and I kept my arms crossed.

He brought his left hand up my side, almost massaging me, and his right hand at my back lowered until he could bunch up the material of my robe in his hand. Those skilled fingers curled against my ass with the motion, and I faltered in my determination to resist him.

"Why?" I asked, sounding too breathy to really appear defensive.

He reached my shoulder and nudged my robe over it. As the fabric slid free, it tickled my skin.

"I think he killed my brother."

I frowned at him. That comment jarred me, snapping me out of this reverie of lust he was too damn good and quick at causing.

"He didn't," I sassed, shaking my head.

He pulled me closer, lowering his hand to my upper arm. Pressure from his fingers built there. I felt no pain, but I refused to be kowtowed into lowering my arms like he suggested.

"You know that?" he challenged. He had a whole fistful of my robe bunched in his hand. The flimsy fabric pulled at my skin, and with the sleeve stuck at my elbow, he took advantage.

Tugging down, he forced the robe to pull my arm back. As soon as I lost that crossed-arm stance, he snaked his arm around me.

The contact of his muscled, hairy arm against my bare flesh fueled me with potent need. With a craving we'd had to pause earlier.

It returned in full force now, taunting me to give in again.

"Because I'm pretty sure you were otherwise preoccupied when someone murdered my brother." He demonstrated a replay of how busy I'd been at that moment—with him. He slammed his lips to mine, kissing me without mercy as he tossed my robe to the floor.

Wrapping my arms around him, I reveled in the press of his lips, hungry and demanding against mine. Arching up into his kiss, I pulled myself flush to him, grinding over his hard body.

I had no restraint. I didn't want any. Kissing Renzo in my room was just as bad of an idea as it was to kiss him in a secluded spot on that patio. And like those blissful short moments, this time was no less drugging and magical.

My pussy was slick once more, aching for his touch to fill me and tease me. I breathed so fast, dizzy with this deep desire. No matter how I reached up to cling to him, I couldn't appease the tense sensation of my nipples, hard and trapped behind the cups of my bra.

I was lost to exploring this forbidden lust with him. As he rendered me weak and needy, chasing after his lips when he pulled back for air, I didn't care.

"He didn't kill Luka," I repeated. It was a crime to be kissing and wanting him, but it was a worse grievance to do so with the thought that he'd come here to accuse my idiotic father.

"You know that?" he growled, dipping to kiss me harder.

When I reared back for air, panting and staring up at him, I implored him to understand. "Why would he have? My father has no reason to kill Luca."

"We're enemies," he reminded me.

I pulled him lower for a hard kiss. "We are."

Even though we're not acting like it at all.

"My father had no reason to care about that wedding, about Luka. At all."

He didn't seem to believe me, but he didn't look prepared to fight the issue. Gripping my ass, he lifted me in his hold. Kissing me and carrying me, he moved me to my bed. We fell together, and before I could reach up to cling to his neck fully, he snapped the elastic band to my thong and tugged the scrap away.

"He was right there," he argued as he slid his hand lower to my pussy. "Your father was right there when it happened."

I groaned at his slow drag, wishing he'd get his fingers inside me faster. Parting my legs, I gave him easy access. When he teased me, stalling with his fingers over my mound and almost tracing my entrance, I whined a helpless whimper and guided him lower.

I pushed his hand down, and once he curled a finger inside me, I let my eyes close at the tight intrusion.

"Nickolas."

He stopped moving. "What?" he bit out.

Shit. I hadn't completed my thought, already so overwhelmed by his touch. His hard tone implied that he didn't want to hear me speak of another man while he was touching me.

"Nickolas must have killed Luka," I added, breathing shallower as he sped up and rubbed against my clit.

He hadn't asked me for my opinion, but if he was here and open enough to tell me his suspicions, then I should be too. This couldn't be normal. Discussing who might have murdered his brother was a weird topic, but debating while he fingered me and kissed down my chest was even stranger.

No. Being able to speak with him—a Mafia man—about "important" matters was an oddity in and of itself.

"Why?" He slowed his fingers, kissing harder as he angled toward my breasts. "Why do you think that?"

"You care what I think?" I tried to keep the smile out of my tone.

He bit the edge of my bra cup and tugged it down. My breast popped out. That hard tip of my nipple pointed at him, and he didn't waste a second to lean closer and suck it into his hot mouth.

"Oh!"

He looked up, glaring at me. "Not so loud."

I replied by reaching for his face and pushing it back to my breast. He resisted, looking up at me. "Why shouldn't I ask you? You're always at the same things we are. You live in this world. You're not an outsider."

He had no clue how much that vote of confidence meant to me. Living with my controlling mother and indifferent father had me assuming I was literally good for nothing, but Renzo wasn't that dismissive.

"Nickolas likely killed your brother because of that old score. I don't remember the details, but they fought over that one whore."

He stared at my breast, watching it sway as he pushed his hand against me, driving his fingers in so deep. "And she ended up dying when she was with Luka, at one of our properties."

I moaned as he sucked my nipple into his mouth again. "Maybe... maybe Nickolas wanted that whore for good and was bitter that he'd lost her to Luka."

"My brother didn't kill her," he argued. "I don't think he did." Then he tugged the other bra cup down, freeing my other breast. Back and forth, he alternated the agony of teasing with his mouth and tongue. Leaning on one elbow, he slanted over me as he pushed me closer and closer to coming. That buildup of tension couldn't last for long, and I reached toward him to get there faster.

"I'm sorry," I got out between quick breaths. "I'm sorry you lost your brother."

He growled, moving up to kiss my mouth soundly. It seemed he didn't want to hear pity. Or sympathy. All he focused on was this intoxicating intimacy we had no business trying to have.

"I wish I could lose it. With you. I want to fuck you hard, Giulia," he growled against my mouth. His dark-blue gaze locked with mine, and I couldn't look away as he pumped and stretched his fingers faster. "I don't want to think about Luka fucking dying." He kissed me harder. "Or that I have to step up to all this bullshit."

I gasped at his thumb circling my clit. "Please."

"I don't want to think about any of these problems. All I want is this," he whispered. "Proving that I can pleasure you and make you come so hard—" He slammed his lips over mine as I did.

I came. With glorious, freeing waves of relief, I lost the fight with that tension. It snapped. I fell apart, splintering under the euphoria of an intense orgasm that I was glad he'd had the foresight to cover my mouth for. He swallowed my loud moans and screams. His lips sealed the sounds I would've unconsciously emitted. If he hadn't muffled me, the guards running through the hallways would've heard and knocked on the door. A lock was never an option here, and Renzo would've been found.

As I caught my breath, staring up at him, he glowered at the closed door.

He might have come here to interrogate my father, but he'd ended up finishing what we'd started.

And he was overstaying his stay.

"Giulia." Francis, one of the lead guards, knocked on my door. "Giulia."

Still glowering at the closed panel of polished wood, Renzo got up smoothly. His fit physique aided him in moving like a ninja, silent and quick. As he lowered to get my robe and thrust it to me, he kept his stare on the door.

"Giulia."

"In a moment," I replied, "I'm indecent."

Renzo smirked at me as I hurried to get my robe on.

"Giulia, open the door before I do," Francis ordered. He wasn't mean about it. I knew he was only doing his job. Even still, I couldn't hurry. My fingers trembled. I felt the fading waves of my orgasm. My pussy was so sensitive, and on my thighs, my cum stuck to my skin.

Renzo took over, pulling the robe over me and tying the sash quickly.

"Giulia," Francis warned.

Renzo dropped to his knees, hiding at my feet on this side of the bed where I stood.

Once he lowered out of sight from the doorway, Francis entered.

I huffed an indignant breath, flustered and alarmed. "What is the meaning of this?" I demanded. My heart raced with Renzo hidden in my room. If they found him, he'd be taken away. If he said a word about accusing my father of murder, he'd be dead.

With a funky sense of déjà vu, I hid him from the guards at the doorway. Francis narrowed his eyes, roving the room, and I crossed my arms and cleared my throat.

"What is the meaning of this?" I demanded.

"Patrol concerns," he replied. "Someone alerted us to a potential intruder."

Too late for that. "Don't you dare wake my sisters."

Francis nodded, still suspicious but appeased enough to leave the room.

I pulled on Renzo's hair, tugging him up.

"Fuck," he hissed at the sting. Catching my hand, he yanked me close for a hard kiss. "You'd better keep your mouth shut about your accusations."

"About Nickolas?" I smirked. "You too. You can't go around telling everyone my father killed Luka."

He growled, kissing me once more. "He's my enemy. *You're* my enemy."

"Yeah, which is why I need your word that you won't tell anyone I was with you outside at the wedding."

He arched one brow, glancing at the bed.

"And that." I bit my lower lip. "Don't tell anyone you were here."

With a final grunt, he kissed me once more. "Why the fuck would I announce that I broke in here at all? I intend to get answers, and I won't be sidetracked by an easy lay."

I shoved at him, annoyed all over again. This hot-and-cold routine was gnawing on my nerves. "That wasn't an 'easy lay'. I'm still a virgin, and that's the way it has to be."

Glowering at me, he shook his head. "I mean it, Giulia. Don't butt into this business about my brother. You keep your thoughts to yourself and don't talk about it."

Is he trying to... protect me? The idea of Renzo wanting to keep me safe felt foreign.

Rushing toward the balcony doors, he left without giving me a chance to demand his silence.

"Renzo!" I hissed, chasing after him as he flung himself over the railing and climbed down.

Spotting guards in the distance, I retreated to the relative security of my room.

One glance at the bed suggested that I'd never feel the same here again.

6

RENZO

Renzo

For the next two days, I had no time to think. I lacked the time to feel anything other than suffocating frustration.

Leaving Giulia the way I had wasn't easy, but those blissful, stolen moments in her room, when I played with her on her bed and made her come so beautifully on my hand, were all that kept me sane in her absence.

In Gio's study, at the warehouse where soldiers and capos met, and in and out of other offices, I was thrust straight into all that Luka once had to handle. While I had been dismissed and free to do as I pleased, he had to speak with all these capos. He had checked in with soldiers. And he'd had his thumb on the pulse of so many secret operations that I felt overwhelmed by it all.

My life was no longer mine. My time was not mine to do with as I saw fit.

I was owned, ruled by the expectations of my father. Without Luka here to deal with all the business, I was screwed.

I didn't begrudge him. He was killed, and I never would have wished him dead for any reason. But at the same time, I felt stuck and spiraling out of control.

If I wasn't listening to the capos explain details to me, I was scrambling to remember who was who. And if I wasn't paying attention to the autopsy that had been done on Luka—confirming that he'd ingested a poison placed in his drink at the wedding reception—I was nodding along and wondering how in the hell my brother had ever handled so many things at once.

No wonder he was such a cold-hearted, aloof asshole.

No wonder he looked vacant and sinister.

He'd never had a chance to live. To just be. And now, it seemed I wouldn't, either.

Instead of mourning his death, Gio and the capos within the Family pushed forward with figuring out who'd killed him. If this was the death of an older member, someone expected to pass away, then yes, preparations would be arranged to celebrate the end of their life with meals, parties, gatherings, and meetings.

No one was celebrating a goddamn thing as the day of Luka's funeral approached. We were all concentrating on identifying the killer. I was fixated on avenging him and killing his murderer. It wasn't shocking that the funeral was to be held so hastily. Respect would be paid later, or as Gio worded it more than once with a nagging tone, *I could pay the ultimate respect by filling his shoes and killing his killer.*

Once I find them, I will.

I drew in a steadying breath as I stood next to my father at the funeral. Aligned with the top leaders and capos, I waited for all the guests to file in.

While none of us were in the mood to grieve Luka and succumb to the loss of a family member, we were alert and eager to see what developments could happen as he was laid to rest. Just like the wedding had been, this grouping of the Mafia's elite could shake loose some clues.

I tracked the entrance of them all. Marcus and Nickolas Romano. Gio nodded at them, greeting them as they arrived, but I beat him to the punch, asking what he had to be struggling to understand.

"Where is Cecilia?" I asked, holding up the line at the entrance to the church. Other guests—minor associates within the Families—filed in around them, perhaps too inferior to suspect that they should pay their respects personally before the ceremony began.

Marcus Romano lifted his chin, eyeing me carefully. Even though he was about the same age as Gio, the Mafia lord looked good. Buff and fit, like he didn't work out for the sake of staying healthy but to remind us all that he could still kick ass.

"She's not here," Nickolas snapped, implying I was an imbecile to inquire.

"Not here?" Gio furrowed his brow. "I don't understand. She wasn't married to him for long, but she was his wife." He gestured toward the altar. Just three days ago, Luka and Cecilia stood at the wide level where a single casket stood waiting now. "How is she not *here*?"

"She's not available," Marcus replied, smoothing down the lapels of his suit.

"Why not?" I persisted. "Where is she?"

"She's not here," Nickolas repeated, tense and impatient.

"I fucking see that. What I don't understand is why she isn't willing to come to her husband's funeral."

Gio shot me a stern look.

"Let us be seated." Marcus dismissed me, looking further into the church and gesturing for Nickolas to go with him. His son wasn't letting it go, though. He narrowed his eyes, seeming to dare me to speak up again.

Once they moved on, Gio caught my gaze and shook his head slightly.

"She married him and can't fucking show up?" I hissed.

"She's always been… delicate."

I huffed, nodding at people as they entered. This tradition of greeting guests before the ceremony didn't make much sense to me, but I appreciated the chance to notice who was where.

And who doesn't bother to show up.

"Delicate. But you wanted Luka to marry her."

"Don't start," Gio warned.

"Is she hiding?" I wondered aloud.

"It hardly matters now."

I squinted at him, amazed that he could be this dumb. Cecilia was the first one who noticed Luka was dead. Of course that woman mattered in all of this.

Before I could speak with him any further, the Acardis arrived.

Isabella held her head up high, scanning the crowds as Rocco sighed. He nodded at me and Gio, a weak acknowledgment of a greeting, but like usual, he didn't seem happy to be there. Giulia followed her parents inside, dipping her chin at me, then Gio.

I bit the inside of my cheek, watching this gorgeous woman as she made brief eye contact with me. That mere glance of her dark-brown gaze heated me up, and all I could think of was how she'd gasped against my mouth when she came. Licking my lips, I fought a growl of need, knowing that this wasn't the time nor place to be fantasizing about tasting her tartly sweet lips again.

This was the first time we'd encountered each other since I snuck out of her room. I had no clue when I'd be able to steal another moment with her again. I was already overtaxed and too busy with this investigation into Luka's death and taking over his role. Being interrupted from playing with her or fucking her sweet pussy was a punishment I didn't want to suffer, but I knew that I couldn't afford the distraction of wanting her.

I had to focus. I had to avenge Luka, and staring at this raven-haired beauty was not going to help that cause at all.

I straightened, severing this pull to stare back at her, and she moved along after her parents.

Telling myself to focus didn't do a damn thing. All through the funeral ceremony, I fought the nagging draw to her. More than once, I caught myself turning her way and hoping to make eye contact. Simply knowing she was near had me on edge, and it became a habitual torture to forbid myself from seeking her out.

At the wake, I struggled even more. She remained near her parents, but without the setting of the church dictating that we pay attention to the priest and the casket holding my brother, it felt like a game to walk past each other without stopping to speak.

Even if I did find a chance to snag her and tug her aside for a private moment, I knew better than to take that risk.

Tensions ran high. Unlike the fake respect people showed at the church, here, over food and drinks, guests seemed looser and more prone to arguing.

No one got along, and as I finally headed toward the bar for a drink, I rubbed my brow and figured war would break out sooner than later.

Aside from the usual scrimmages and disagreements that always peppered the conversations in our world, accusations continued to be flung all over the place. No one was coming out and accusing anyone of killing Luka, but lips were loose. People talked.

And *everyone* made sure to keep their drinks close and covered with their hands. I couldn't blame them for being nervous after the heir to the Bernardi wealth was assassinated at the last party.

Nothing new was learned, though. All through the wake, Gio and I conversed with many. We both checked in with the capos who were listening and sneaking around. This wasn't just a send-off or mock celebration for Luka's life. It was an opportunity to spy and learn who might have killed him.

Nothing. That was what we learned. A fat load of nothing. All the guests remained on edge, and the overall vibe of the gathering was one of anxiety.

Nickolas and Rocco fell prey to the tension first. I wasn't near them when they broke into a fight, but two capos stood by in the parking lot as the men used their fists on each other.

And that was why when Giulia approached the bar, I sympathized with the fatigue and irritation shown on her expressive face.

The whole afternoon and evening, I did my best to avoid her, but I didn't move away when she made it clear that she was coming for a drink. She looked like she needed it.

"Are they done out there?" I asked, mildly interested.

She sighed, shaking her head slightly. "I think so." Casting a glance over her shoulder, she grimaced. "I don't even want to know what that was about."

I shrugged. "Tensions are high."

"And Nickolas is an angry asshole who always wants to fight someone over something."

I nodded, entertained that she knew this. He was my peer, and it was common knowledge that Nickolas Romano was a hothead. But no woman—no properly obedient and quiet Mafia daughter—would ever share her opinion like that so freely.

Except her.

"My mother's going to be furious, nagging at him all night for 'dragging down the Acardi name,'" she groused.

"She doesn't like it when he fights?" I guessed.

"She doesn't like it when he fights and everyone sees how weak and old he is and that he loses."

Fair enough. It wasn't a pretty image. Then again, if Nickolas offended Rocco, the man would have to stand up and fight back.

I couldn't ignore how easily she confided in me. While I suspected she might only be freer with her words because we'd succumbed to lust, I knew I had to take advantage anyway.

Giulia knew the same people I did. She might not realize the worth of the nuggets of information people might share around her. Like the other women and daughters of our world, she filed into the background, submissive and not expected to have her own thoughts. If she overheard anything, something people might be too nervous to tell *me*...

"Giulia. We need to talk." I slid my forearms along the bar top, edging closer to her without looking up and facing her. She caught on, not glancing at me either. We had to speak but not let anyone realize that we were. We *were* enemies, or at least our Families were.

"For fuck's sake, Renzo. Here? Now?"

"Where's Cecilia?" I whispered as I brought my glass to my lips, hiding the movement of my mouth in case anyone was watching us.

She stiffened. "What?"

"Where is Cecilia? Have you heard?"

Through my peripheral vision, I watched her frown. "I thought you'd want to talk about..."

"No." I didn't want to talk about how good she felt or gloat about proving her wrong, that I was thoroughly capable of pleasuring a woman—pleasuring her. If I had my way, I'd prefer to repeat that action, to steal her away and fuck her like I've been fantasizing about since the moment I first touched her pussy on the patio.

I dared to look at her, letting her see the desire I doubted I'd ever be able to dial down for her.

She swallowed. Her throat flexed with the force of that motion, and I felt triumphant to know I'd unsettled her and had gotten her this flustered.

"I don't... know." She cleared her throat again, dropping back into this secret conversation.

If she were any other woman, she'd fuss and insist that we talk about what we did or put me on the spot to demand more. Something. But she understood the assignment. I was only speaking to her to get intel, and she wasn't going to withhold it or use that against me.

"She's not here," she added as she lifted her glass to also cover up what she said.

I know that. "I am capable of making that observation on my own."

"But I heard a few asking about *where* she is. My mother is very curious about it too."

I risked another direct glance at her, raising one brow. This was going somewhere now. Isabella Acardi always snooped in other people's business.

"She's been asking and gossiping," she replied. "And it seems like many think Cecilia ran away and is hiding."

"Where—"*Fuck.* I caught a reflection in a bottle on the bar's shelves, and it was enough to make me shut up and leave. *Speak of the devil.* Isabella Acardi was coming straight for her.

Without finishing my conversation with Giulia, I was wrenched away from her once more.

I didn't want to be caught talking with the enemy, and I didn't want this woman to know I was sort of using her daughter as a secret source of intel, either. Keeping my distance from Isabella was necessary, but at the same time, I loathed how it kept me away from her daughter whom I craved.

After I left Giulia to deal with her mother, I ran into *my* parent. Gio stopped me in the hallway leading to the restrooms, and I sighed. I was exhausted of his presence. He wasn't leaning on me for emotional support. I was just the shove-in, the replacement for the heir he'd lost. From a life of never speaking to him, out of sight and out of mind, this was a heavy adjustment to get used to.

"You need to figure out who killed Luka," he reminded me.

I clenched my jaw, furious with his nagging.

I know!

I didn't need him to tell me again. It went without saying that I'd be expected to avenge my brother. Regardless of how we'd never been close, I would never sit back and slack in this duty.

"I am counting on you to seek justice for him," he growled. "And the sooner you can tell me that you've taken care of his killer, the better you can move forward as my next-in-line."

I was sick of this. I knew. I didn't require any more instructions, and I shoved away from him, desperate to have a moment to myself.

7

GIULIA

Giulia

The funeral for Luka lasted well into the evening. I wasn't sure how Renzo was able to hold up with it all. He seemed so distracted and moody throughout the funeral and the wake. Instead of looking sad and grieving, he seemed annoyed.

More than once, I noticed him checking me out. While I felt giddy that I'd ensnared his attention, I knew better than to entertain anything happening between us. I'd begged him to not tell anyone about what we'd done together. He had to lie along with me.

Still, my mother honed in on my sitting next to him. She'd pass out in shame if she knew I was telling Renzo about what she was gossiping about at Luka's funeral, that she was trying to get juicy drama about Cecilia being missing. We weren't the only ones curious about why the new bride wasn't at her husband's funeral, but no one had any actual facts to share. Only speculation.

"I don't even want to see you near that man," she scolded as she told me to get ready to leave.

She'd finished harassing my father for "letting himself get into another fight", this time, with Nickolas. I wasn't sure what started it all, but I was grateful that my younger sisters hadn't come to the funeral.

Everyone seemed on edge at the funeral, and Nickolas was no exception. Maybe the Romano son was still suspicious of Father being near Cecilia when Luka was dead. Whatever the reason, whatever sparked the embers of violence, they'd fought. Mother was furious about the crass and ridiculous display, and it was only after she'd gotten him to be taken to the car that she sought me out.

At least Renzo was smart enough to leave.

I let her rants go in one ear and out the other. The whole ride home, she complained. She bitched. And she got on to my father again, lambasting him for trying to act like a macho man half his age.

After I helped my sisters to bed, tiredly telling them that they didn't need to concern themselves with why our parents were arguing—again—I headed to my room and paced.

Being near Renzo stirred something within me. That desire he'd flamed and fanned in this very room was turning into a persistent, nagging need, but I had to stop this nonsense. Nothing could ever happen between us, and I was stunned by how much that concept bothered me.

All this time, all those years, I didn't concern myself with Renzo Bernardi. He was there, always in the background, but now, he was at the forefront of my mind.

As I lay in bed, wondering about where he was and what he was doing, I thought back to how he'd reacted since his brother was killed. Renzo was a playboy, chasing easy pussy and doing whatever he wanted. Since he was no longer the spare brother but next in line to take over the Bernardi name, he had to be struggling.

And if he was suffering from the changes in his life…

I want to be the one to comfort him and support him.

"Stop this," I whispered to myself as I closed my eyes.

Dreaming about being Renzo's partner was stupid. Nonsense. Our being together would never, ever make sense in our world. Too many years had passed with our Families hating each other. Yet as I drifted closer to sleep, I wished to feel him on this bed again, his lips hard against mine and his hands holding me tightly.

When I woke, it was too soon and because of my mother's phone. It rang and rang, over and over again.

"What the hell..."

My room wasn't near hers, and when I said *hers*, it was only hers. Father often slept in another bedroom, and if that wasn't representative of how poorly they got along, I wasn't sure what else could be.

The trill repeated without pause, and as I lay in bed, staring at the ceiling and damning the noise that came far too early, I realized she was likely still sleeping in and had forgotten it up here.

I growled, leaving my room to shut off the device. I didn't have to search for it. With a frown, I looked down and stared at it. Right there in the hallway. Her cell phone lay buzzing and lighting up with an alarm clock going off, over and over and over.

"Oh, shut up," I muttered as I stooped to pick it up.

Maybe she dropped it? Or it fell out of her pocket? I didn't care. I just wanted quiet to sleep a little longer.

I held the device and looked both ways up and down the hall. Marianna, Beatrice, and Lucia stayed in rooms further down the corridor, but Father's "room" was nearer.

How am I the only one who heard this? It hadn't stopped in all those five or ten minutes when I tried to lie in and go back to sleep.

Heading toward their rooms, I yawned and bemoaned how terribly I'd slept. Thinking about Renzo threw me off. Missing his touch and yearning for his kisses kept me antsy, and wondering about who killed his brother intrigued me.

I knocked and opened the door to their master bedroom, surprised that Father was actually in the bed for once. Mother wasn't there, though, but I figured she couldn't have been up for long.

"Father?" I called out as I entered. Although he liked to drink—a lot, and often—he was often one of the first ones awake in the household. When I was younger, when Lucia and Beatrice were still toddlers, I realized that he rose from bed early so he could have an hour or two of silence to himself in the house. My sisters were no longer that young, but it seemed that the habit stuck.

Until today.

"Father?" I asked again, furrowing my brow as I approached the bed.

He didn't stir.

At all.

I stopped and stared at him as another, bigger realization hit me.

He's not snoring. He always did.

But he wasn't now.

"Father?" I hurried to his side of the bed and studied him closer. A scream built in my throat. It remained trapped there, lodged without any escape. My heart raced as I tried to comprehend what my eyes were suggesting. That my father, so still and unmoving—not breathing—might be…

"Father." I shook him, feeling the lifelessness of his weight being pushed. "Oh, *fuck*." I shoved at him harder, moving one hand to hover over his face. No air huffed up. His chest didn't rise and fall. With shaking fingers, I laid my hand over him, waiting for a telltale *thump-thump* of a heartbeat to reach my skin.

Nothing. He wasn't breathing. His heart had stopped.

I choked on air, stuttering to breathe through this shock. "Dead?" I whispered, shaking him harder one last time. His hand fell off his stomach, flopping to the mattress with a weight that couldn't be denied.

"Oh, fuck." I staggered backward, staring at him as horror and dread consumed me. Dizzy and scared, I almost tripped on my own feet. But I managed to turn and run.

"Francis!" I shouted, hoping he was the patroller on duty near this wing of the mansion. He usually was, but I couldn't bank on normalcy. Nothing about finding my father dead this morning was "usual".

"Francis!" I tried once more, louder, no longer worried about waking anyone else up. With this eerie feeling of being so alone up here, I needed to see another person. "Mother! Francis!" I called out for them, frantic for someone to reply.

When Beatrice stepped out of her room, I held my hand up and told her to go back to bed. "No. Just stay in your room until I come to you."

Lucia opened her door and poked her head out too. "Giulia? What's happening?"

Marianna showed too, snapping to attention. I could only imagine how tense I looked, but whatever expression she saw on my face, it prompted her to listen. "Come on. Let's wait in my room." She tossed a worried glance over her shoulder at me as she ushered Beatrice and Lucia into her room.

"Mother!" I ran down to her room as the sound of guards and soldiers rushed through the house.

"Mother—" I stopped short after flinging her door open. She lay on the floor, face-down. The pale-pink carpet cut a sharp contrast to the blue of her nightgown, but I saw at once that she lived. Lying on her arm, with it trapped under her stomach, she reclined in an awkward position that emphasized how her chest still rose and fell.

She was breathing. She was alive.

"Mother!" I dropped to my knees and rolled her over quickly, seeing that she was out of it, but breathing.

"Miss Giulia," a guard said, announcing his arrival as he rushed into the room. As soon as he noticed my mother on the floor, I backed up.

"She's asleep." I shook my head as I slapped her face. Then I shook her. As the guards filed in, I let them try to rouse her too. "She was asleep on the floor. I found her like this. But—"

Shouts sounded from across the hall. They'd found him. "Father's dead," I told the guard still trying to revive my mother.

He pressed his fingers to her pulse point, nodding. "She's got a pulse. Stay back, please."

I scrambled back, staring wide-eyed as they took over. We employed a medic, but that was it. More and more soldiers and guards entered the room. In the hall, they hurried to the master suite to deal with my father.

In the frenzy of too many actions, all the men speaking and working as a team, I tried to follow what they decided and instructed.

Securing the premises. Taking my mother to the hospital. Guarding my father's body. Checking on who else could have been hurt.

"Giulia."

I whipped around at Uncle Dario's voice. He hurried with his cane the best he could, and I ran to him, helping him stand steady.

"What's going on?"

"Father is dead. It seems that Mother was drugged."

He frowned down at me. "Drugged?"

I was guessing there, but I had no other instant idea coming to mind. She was alive. I saw no signs of an outward injury. "I don't know, but—"

"Just now?"

He turned to Francis as he rushed up to us, relaying the basic facts that my mother would be transported to the hospital now.

"Giulia?" Marianna called from her room.

I winced, running to her and keeping her in her room.

"What's going on?" all three of them asked as I stepped inside Marianna's safe haven.

"I'll tell you…" *Later.* I didn't want to break the news to them, but they had to know one way or another.

"Your father is dead," Uncle Dario answered for me when I hesitated. He came into the room, hugging Lucia as she cried out.

"Is Mother…?" Marianna's eyes bugged out.

"No. She's breathing," I told her. "But I found Father dead and Mother lying on the floor. They're taking her to the hospital now."

At the news that one of our parents was dead and the other was unconscious and needing medical assistance, the trio of sisters reacted with tears, shocked gasps, and so many blurted, panicked questions. None of which I could answer. I'd only discovered this hell this morning, and with Dario's help, I tried to keep them as calm and safe as possible.

Francis directed the guards. They rushed through the house. I heard them shouting outside. When they weren't, their fingers were lifted to their earpieces as they conversed with each other.

Dario hobbled out of Marianna's room, leaving me with them and expecting me to do my best to calm them.

No one was calm. How could they be? Waking to this news rocked us all. I *looked* cool and collected, but it was a sham, a brave front I put on for the sake of my sisters crying and clinging to me as they struggled with this double discovery.

Uncle Dario was furious, raising his voice at Francis and the other guards. Through the door, I caught every angry word he flung at the men who were supposed to protect this home. He demanded answers, expecting someone to report in with evidence of someone breaking in to kill my father and drug my mother.

Word came back quickly that she seemed fine. Drowsy and still loopy under the doctor's care, but alive.

I didn't want to know what they did with Father's body, and when they wheeled him out of there, I turned my head and ordered my uncle to shut the door after him. We didn't need the girls to witness his being removed from the house.

Marianna was sullen and quiet, likely reverting inside and clamming up. She helped, though, hugging Lucia and holding Beatrice's hand. We weren't orphaned. Mother lived, but without our father at the head of the Family, it dawned on me that we were in dire straits.

We were just at a funeral yesterday, and now we'd woken to more death. Death at home. On our turf.

As I listened to Dario speaking with the guards again, I thought back to Renzo's reaction to the death in his Family. I'd never thought of the Bernardi brothers as close siblings. Not like I was with my sisters. If one of them had passed away, I wouldn't have been able to remain this calm and level-headed, even though I was so shaken and bewildered, confused and nervous.

Renzo hadn't cried and freaked out at Luka's death. All I could discern was that he wanted to seek justice. To find the killer.

That burning need to avenge my father's death hadn't sunk in, and I wasn't sure when or if it would. Shock kept me from being motivated to *do* anything yet, and I felt guiltier not to be sadder.

I'd never been close with my father, but I already felt the depth of his loss.

He was, for better or worse, a source of security. The patriarch. The head of the Family and the Boss of the Acardi organization.

Without him…

Freedom wouldn't come. I felt too lost and disoriented to know what would happen next, and at the realization of accepting the unknowns that would come, I missed Renzo even more.

Stupid as it was, I wished he were here. That he could just be here and look at me with that sharp, yet adoring, gaze he seemed to save just for me. How he'd gaze at me with challenge but respect. He didn't scold me like my mother did. He didn't dismiss me like my father had. And he didn't merely leer at me like a pervert like all the other men did.

Renzo looked upon me with something like reluctant acceptance, and I wished I could lean on him and soak in the security of his presence now.

"Fucking Bernardi."

I whipped up from zoning out at the wall. Uncle Dario breathed heavily as he entered the living room hours later. We'd eventually all gotten dressed, but the day was too skewed to do much else. My sisters were in Marianna's room, napping or just lying together after a late lunch no one had really touched.

Uncle Dario sought me out in the library, though, furious and worked up emotionally and physically as he labored his steps to the sofa.

"What?" I stood, hurrying to help him sit.

"Bernardi." He winced as he lowered to the cushion. "He fucking killed Rocco."

I'd *just* been thinking about Renzo Bernardi in a forbidden, wistful way. How could my uncle be speaking about the same man in such a different manner? "What?"

"I heard him." He glared absently, shaking his head. "At the funeral. I heard him."

I sat next to him, desperate for an explanation. Mother and Father never shared information with me freely, but Uncle Dario never seemed to mind. He'd often called me the only level-headed adult in this house. "You heard who say what?"

"Renzo." He met my gaze, showing me the anger there. "Renzo Bernardi killed your father."

"And drugged Mother?" I shook my head. "No. I can't see it. That's not…"

"I heard him."

"You heard *what*?" I insisted, unafraid to raise my voice with him. Uncle Dario never played games with my head.

"Giovanni and his son. I heard them at the funeral. He insisted that Renzo kill whoever murdered Luka."

I reared back, alarmed as I stared at him. "What? Hold on. Are you saying that Father killed Luka?"

He grimaced. "No. Of course, Rocco didn't kill Luka."

I narrowed my eyes. He seemed so sure. "How do you know?"

"Because Rocco is—was—a spineless coward. He never would've had the balls to kill a highly regarded man like Luka, even if he was our Family's rival."

I agreed.

"Why would he have?" Uncle Dario said with a wry huff. "What would Rocco gain from killing Luka?"

That was exactly what I told Renzo that night he came here to speak with Father. As far as I knew, he never did speak with him. Since that night when Luka was killed, I hadn't seen Renzo—not until the funeral.

Renzo seemed to change his mind, anyway. When we talked, or argued, before he made me come, he'd appeared to come to terms with my rationalization. He only accused my father of killing Luka because he had been close to the head table when Luka was found dead, and that wasn't a strong argument to begin with. If anything, it seemed like Renzo had left with the consideration that Marcus or Nickolas Romano had likely killed Luka.

"I'd be accusing Nickolas before Renzo," I said, thinking back to how the younger Romano had fought my father at the funeral.

Uncle Dario shook his head. "No. Nickolas fights anyone he can. Just because he and Rocco fought earlier doesn't mean anything."

I'm not so sure about that.

"I can't ignore what I heard, Giulia." He implored me with an intense stare, begging me to heed his words wisely. "I *just* heard Giovanni telling Renzo to avenge Luka. And now Rocco is dead."

I pressed my lips together, unable to persuade him to drop that line of thought. No, that line of assumptions. Renzo and I had talked about the possibility of my father being Luka's killer, and I refused to think he would have changed his mind enough to come out and just kill Father like this.

And why would he poison Mother, too?

Nothing was adding up, and I was stuck to keeping my encounters with Renzo private. The last thing I needed on top of all this trouble and drama was anyone suggesting I was no longer a pure virgin to be married off.

"Let's not rush to any assumptions," I warned him gently.

"Are you defending Renzo?" he demanded sharply.

Shit. I could see how he'd notice my line of argument and get curious.

"No." *Yes.* I licked my lips, searching for something better to say. "Let's just calm down first. We'll wait to see what Mother says. What comes up as the men search and watch the surveillance of the property."

He nodded, but the tight scowl on his face suggested he wouldn't relax anytime soon. Just like I had, he'd lost his leader. The head of the Acardi Family was gone, and without any guidance, we would all feel lost.

I had no clue what was coming next, but I could count on one awful fact.

With my uncle so quick to assume Renzo killed my father, I would never have a chance to spend time with my sexy enemy again. His rash words promised that I wouldn't be able to look forward to being in Renzo's company, no matter how much he hogged my attention and stayed in my mind.

Renzo couldn't have killed Father.

I wanted to swear on it.

Because if he had, I'd lost my chance to know the exquisite pleasure that man—my enemy—could evoke in me.

And it felt like a crueler loss that I wouldn't be able to overcome.

8

RENZO

Renzo

Two days after Luka's funeral, Gio called me into his study.

I steadied my breath, trying to be patient as I headed there. He'd been on my ass all week with the same order—find Luka's killer. As if I could've forgotten. And that was all I'd fucking done. The day after the funeral, I was on the road and speaking with capos. Checking in with everyone in the organization, both to let them know I was in charge now and would take the role seriously and to investigate who could have killed my brother.

Yesterday, I was doing more of the same. I'd lost too many hours speaking with a supposed spy the men had caught. He'd been playing a game with us, pretending that he knew valuable details about what really happened the night of Luka and Cecilia's wedding, but he was just bluffing, trying to earn a little money.

Stupid.

No one bribed *us* and won. Once we realized he was messing with us and didn't have any intel to identify Luka's killer, I had the soldiers torture him until he begged for death.

I didn't have time to deal with fools like that, and I didn't have the patience to deal with my father now. But I went to see him regardless.

"You called?" I greeted.

"Rocco Acardi is dead." He steepled his fingers together and eyed me closely.

What. The. Fuck? I froze, refusing to give away any indication of shock. I was a quick learner. In this position of being the next in line to rule the Bernardi Family, I couldn't ever let anyone see what I was feeling. It was a hard lesson to acclimate to. I enjoyed being human, fun-loving and reckless. Now, I had to perfect that stupid blank mask I'd always hated on Luka.

"Dead?"

He nodded. "According to Isabella Acardi, he was killed."

I sat, unable to look away. "What do you mean, *according to Isabella?*"

"She claims he was killed, but for fuck's sake, Rocco wasn't aging well."

"How'd he die?" It had to include suspicious circumstances to have a debatable cause of death.

"Cardiac arrest."

I narrowed my eyes. Just like Luka had, officially. The autopsy showed traces of poison in my brother's blood, and he was too young and fit to croak from a natural cause like a heart attack.

Rocco wasn't. He indulged in food and alcohol. He was winded in fights, out of shape.

"I've never trusted that woman," Gio said roughly. "I wouldn't put it past her if Rocco died naturally but she wanted to use the news to her advantage."

"How?" Without Rocco, Dario would be the de-facto leader. But he was younger and handicapped, not a leader figure like Rocco had been.

Damn, Giulia. Instead of wondering how Isabella was handling and twisting the loss of her husband, I quickly grew worried about how Giulia was taking the death of her father.

"To sow doubts. To incite drama." Gio rolled his eyes. "To insist on sympathy. Having your spouse killed gains more respect than telling everyone about what a weak, old fool they were to die in their sleep."

"Speaking of spouses dying," I said, "where the fuck is Cecilia?"

He sighed. "No one knows."

I grunted. "Fucking hell, Gio. She's your daughter-in-law."

"Was," he argued. "For all of a goddamn hour."

I tilted my head to the side, not understanding his stance on her absence. "Still, you can't ask Marcus where the hell she is?"

He narrowed his eyes, seeming annoyed that I'd talk back. "You. You ask Marcus. Better yet, ask Nickolas. I'll need you to meet with him soon about a drug trade he and Luka were arranging."

I sighed, nodding and rubbing my brow. Business, business, business. No wonder Luka was a dead-eyed zombie. He never had a chance to live. I hadn't taken a break from all these duties since they were thrust on me, and all I wanted to do if I could have a moment alone was explore this desire Giulia had instilled in me.

After all these days, I missed her. She's come to matter too damn much, and as I realized my thoughts were wandering back to her, to the memories of her kisses and her surrender, I knew I had to stop it all.

Now, of all times, I couldn't be distracted. Gio would only nag me more the longer it took me to find Luka's killer.

I wanted to reach out to her and check on her, but I couldn't afford to do so with any personal interest. "Did they have a funeral? For Rocco?"

Gio shook his head. "Isabella wanted it to be a private affair."

I checked my phone, standing and prepared to take off—again—to speak with a soldier who'd been spying on someone who'd stolen from us recently. "Is that all?" I asked. I wasn't sure why Gio wanted to personally tell me that Rocco had been killed.

"Did you kill him?"

I slanted my eyebrows, squinting at him. "What?"

"Did you kill Rocco?" he asked.

"No."

He smirked. "Figures."

"What the fuck does that mean?"

"I expect you to find Luka's killer. And for a moment, when I heard about this, I got my hopes up that you'd done it."

I rolled my eyes. After talking with Giulia, I saw how stupid it was to assume Rocco was the killer. "If I had, I would've been sure to get his confession to it, then told you as soon as it was done."

He shrugged. "A man can only hope."

"Hope for what?" *Stop talking in fucking riddles.*

"That you're not as worthless as you've always been. That when I ask you to avenge your brother, you will."

I didn't reply, leaving him and wishing I could punch that smug sneer right off his face. It wasn't my fault that he had this low opinion of me.

He'd made sure to dismiss me my whole life, and now I had to redefine myself on the spot.

At the club where I was supposed to meet with the man who'd have intel for me, I grabbed a drink and waited for twenty minutes. The man texted, saying he was on the trail of that guy again, and I sighed, realizing I'd been sitting here for no reason all this time.

It wasn't wasted, though. I killed the time by looking up news about Rocco's death, unsurprised when I didn't find much. Like anyone else in the Mafia world, Isabella knew how to manipulate the news. And it seemed she had.

I left, still looking at my phone as I overheard Nickolas Romano entering the club. It was on neutral ground, not a Bernardi or Romano establishment, but I perked up when he mentioned Giulia's name.

"Now that Rocco's out of the way, I could," he said to another man walking into the club with him.

Can what? I ducked to the side of the hall, sticking with the shadows to listen in.

"You'd do that?" the other man asked.

Nickolas huffed a laugh. "Yeah. I could take over the Acardi Family by marrying Giulia."

They headed in while I left, and as I walked to my car, I mulled over that idea.

Nickolas Romano marrying Giulia Acardi. It left a nasty taste in my mouth. I hated the thought of that fucker claiming her virginity. Of taking her like I now wanted to. I'd always been aware of her beauty, but it was only since we'd both snapped to the attraction between us that I became obsessed with having her.

"Forget about it," I mumbled to myself.

Nickolas would marry her if he saw a benefit to it. And what could I do about it? Not a single fucking thing. She'd be arranged in a marriage someday, and it wouldn't be to me. We were all subject to being married off, pawns for alliances, and there was no way in hell my father would suggest I marry Isabella's daughter.

I got into my car and came face to face with her. Or rather, face to reflection. I held my breath and narrowed my eyes at Giulia sitting in the backseat of my car.

"What the…?" I looked at her, worried. "How the fuck did you get in here?"

"I taught myself to pick locks when I was six years old."

Impressive. She must have been a bored child.

"*Why* are you here?"

She sighed, sinking against the seat. I didn't have to be a genius to see that she needed a moment. Hell, I did too. Hearing Nickolas make plans to conquer her and have her as his wife didn't sit well with me. Knowing she'd sought *me* out mattered.

But what do you want?

I'd parked in the corner. No one could see in here with the tinted windows, and I marveled at the fact that she knew which car was mine.

She'd been aware of me all this time too, and it sucked that we were crashing too close together now when there was no chance of anything happening.

When she sighed, glancing out the window, I bit my lip and got out.

Was she sad? Mad? Lost and confused? She wasn't supposed to matter. I wasn't supposed to care. But I did. I got out of the driver's seat and got into the back with her, facing her profile.

"Aren't you supposed to be all important now, taking Luka's position and having a driver to take you everywhere?"

I scooted in closer. *"That's* why you broke into my car to talk to me?" Her scent hit me hard, enticing me to grab her and hold her close. Her bold gaze threatened to make me lose my mind.

All I wanted was her, a chance to be alone with her, but I knew it was wrong. Now that we were in this private bubble, shrouded and hidden in my car, I wasn't sure how to approach. Or whether I should.

Her silent stare unnerved me, and that damn worry crept back in. She looked so confused, so troubled, and I wanted to smooth away every worry in her mind. Never had I wanted to take care of a woman so badly, and she was the last one on earth I should be staring at and fighting back this possessive, protective streak over.

"Did you kill my father?" she asked bluntly.

I rolled my eyes. "No."

"How can I trust you?"

I shrugged. "You can't."

She licked her lips, staring at my mouth. "I trusted you to prove yourself to me before."

In making her come. Fuck. She was trouble.

"Now's not a good time," I warned.

But her face fell. That sad, mad, and confused frown deepened as she crawled closer and straddled me. I set my hands on her hips, then her ass, as she settled on top of my lap. When she looped her arms around my neck and hugged me tightly, I furrowed my brow, at a loss for what was going on.

"We will never have a good time," she whispered.

You got that right.

I rubbed my hands up her back, stunned that she would be so bold as to seek comfort from me. And that I would want to provide it. As she drew in a shaky breath, I held her tighter and gripped her back to keep her flush to me.

"I didn't kill Rocco," I told her. It mattered that she knew that. "I was at the bar with Gio and my relatives well into the night after the funeral."

She sighed, leaning on me and pressing all of her sweet curves to me.

I rubbed her back, relishing this almost peaceful moment she'd insisted on so stubbornly. Asking her if she was all right would be stupid. She couldn't be. Her father had died, and now she was vulnerable. "Giulia?"

"Hmm."

"Did your father engage in any talks about your marriage?"

She leaned back, staring at me with a scowl. "No. At least, not that I know of." Setting her hands on my shoulders, she cast her gaze down. "Besides, he wouldn't have cared or had any say in it. My mother is scheming. She'll be the one to choose my fate. Father never cared about anything."

I watched her trace her fingers over the buttons of my shirt, absent and listless about it, like she couldn't sit still.

"All he wanted to do was drink and get away from my mother and his daughters." She looked up at me, pinning me with a sober stare. "I found him that morning." Her throat flexed with a tense swallow. "And I had to make the arrangements for his private funeral."

I saw how much she'd been through, and with Isabella as a mother, she would've been on her own through it all. For her sisters, too. While Giulia didn't seem sad about her father's death, she was stressed. And worried.

Seeing her so concerned bothered me. It excited me that she'd been so desperate to see me that she broke into my car just to talk, but I hated what I'd overheard.

Should I tell her? Will she appreciate the heads up that Nickolas is trying to take over her Family now?

"And all I wanted was... to feel safe again. Like I do when I'm near you." She sighed, letting her shoulders slump as she gazed at me with such longing that I wanted to growl.

"That's stupid."

"I know." She halfheartedly flicked her finger between us. "We're enemies."

Doesn't feel like it, does it? The warmth between her legs made me harder. Feeling her weight over my dick threatened to change the course of this topic.

But I reined in my lust. I fought it, wrangling it back into control because neither of us could handle the curveball of wanting each other.

I framed her face and pulled her close to kiss her brow. Giving a tender kiss wasn't my style. Giulia's vulnerability shouldn't have been my kryptonite.

Which was why all I could tell her was this sincere warning. "You need to stay away from me. From looking into Luka's death, and your father's. You need to stay out of it, Giulia."

Beneath the sadness and longing burning in her eyes, I saw the curiosity that wouldn't quit.

That would only promise more worries.

And more trouble.

9

GIULIA

Giulia

"Stay out of it?" I smirked. "Too late for that."

It felt so natural to climb onto his lap. I gravitated toward Renzo, and it made my heart sing with rare happiness that he didn't protest, ward me off, or ask what the hell I thought I was doing, seeking his comfort. He *got* me. And I knew not many others would.

"What do you mean?" He furrowed his brow, rubbing his fingers back and forth on the small of my back.

We'd leapt from enemies to, well, something else, but this easygoing camaraderie, this closeness without the feral lust, was even better.

I hadn't taken the risk to sneak into his car just to straddle him and get a hug. That was an unexpected bonus I hadn't known I'd ask for. Nor that he'd give it so freely.

I'd come to talk about my father's death. Hearing him suggest that Father's passing could have been involved with a marriage arrangement for me made me pause. Narrowing my eyes, I shelved the news I had planned to tell him. "Who was my father supposed to talk about my marriage with?"

He sighed, and I worried that he'd clam up with that slight hesitation, but he didn't. "Nickolas Romano."

I cringed, unable to hide it.

"I know."

"You know what?" I snapped.

"Your face said it all. Being married to him would be…"

"Hell?" I finished for him. Nickolas was a sadist, an abusive asshole, always spoiling for a fight. I rolled my eyes. "Being a woman in our world is already hell."

He licked his lips and nodded, watching me closely. "Not many choices, are there?"

Unless I want to try to run away from it all. I'd considered it before. But now wasn't the time to mess with wistful thoughts. "Are you implying that Nickolas could have killed my father?"

"He did just fight him at my brother's funeral."

"Nickolas fights people all the time," I reminded him.

"As I left that club, I overheard him saying he could marry you and take over the Acardis."

I dropped my head, groaning, and he hugged me close until I was flush against his chest again. Turning to rest my cheek on him, I let his heartbeat soothe my frantic mind. "My uncle is worried about the same thing. Without a patriarch, without my father, we're vulnerable."

He rubbed my back, nodding.

"My mother still isn't herself either, drugged up and acting confused."

He pushed me up to stare into my eyes. "What?"

"My mother." I frowned. He hadn't been surprised by the news that Father was dead. Word had spread, regardless of Mother trying to control what was said. But it seemed like no one knew she'd been drugged too. "I found her at the same time, unconscious but alive." He let me fall against him, and soon, he rubbed my back again, calming me enough to continue. Of all places to find solace, it was in the arms of my enemy. "My whole family is practically coming apart, and Uncle Dario and I won't be the only ones who are aware of how easy it would be to take over us all. Nickolas isn't slow to realize it either."

But I'd rather die than be married off to him. I curled my fingers into Renzo's shirt, clutching him tightly.

"There's no head of the Family anymore, and aligning with me, marrying me, would secure the end of the Acardi rule."

Renzo sighed, shaking his head. "But why bother? The Romanos don't need the Acardi name. You're not their rival."

Nor were the Bernardis. "It would eliminate us as a separate power."

He chuckled. "Have you always been this strategic and observant?"

I knew not many other young women were. And why should they pay attention? Our fates all ended the same, married off and possessed by the man who'd use us as they saw fit. "More or less. What else is there to do than wait for my marriage, then roll over for some asshole who'd want to make me pop out babies?"

He growled, lifting my face with two of his fingertips under my chin. His mouth smashed against mine, and the instant hit of arousal made my pussy clench with need.

"I don't want to think about you rolling over for anyone," he said.

"Except you?" I teased, wondering if he'd admit it. Renzo had made his life nothing but a party, living wild and chasing women.

He groaned, kissing me hard again. I leaned into his kiss, slanting into his hungry touch, but I knew I couldn't forget what I'd come here for. Besides his comfort. Kissing him, with me seated on top of him like this, would quickly slip into this desire that I wasn't sure I could restrain for long.

I reared back, smoothing my hand over his jaw. He breathed hard, glaring at me as though he damned me for backing off. He proved his worth, though, and didn't demand that I kiss him again.

He wouldn't be just another asshole to dominate me. He'd do so in a way I craved, but I'd never find out.

"I don't want to talk about my having to marry anyone," I said. As I licked my lips, tasting him still, he squeezed my ass.

"Me neither." He scowled, staring at my mouth like he hated being held back from temptation. "Besides, I don't know if Isabella would allow you to marry into the Romanos."

I huffed. "Yeah, right. She's already super cautious about trying to stay in Marcus's favor."

"But then she'd need to answer to someone else. It seems like she's always worn the pants in your family. She bossed Rocco around, and if you married into a higher power like the Romanos, she'd lose that."

I nodded, but the gesture evolved into a shrug. "That's not what I wanted to talk about, though. That's not why I snuck in here to see you."

He pulled me over the hardness beneath his pants, and I hissed quickly at the delicious friction I wanted more of.

"You want to *talk?*" he taunted, kissing my neck then licking up toward my ear.

I shivered and pushed his chest until he slumped back in the seat. "Yes. And it'll suggest that you shut the fuck up about telling me to stay out of this business." I slanted him a stern look, knowing I was crossing significant boundaries to tell him this. "Luka was drugged."

He frowned.

"And so was my father. And Mother."

"What are you suggesting?"

"I'm not 'suggesting' anything. Dario overheard the men talking with my mother at the hospital while she recovered. It sounds like the same thing that Luka was given when he died."

He narrowed his eyes, pensive.

"Whoever gave my parents that poison did the same thing to Luka." That connection was a huge detail that I struggled to keep to myself. Knowing how badly Renzo wanted to find his brother's killer, I was pushed to tell him what I'd learned.

"You swear on this?"

I nodded. "I didn't hear it myself, but yes. Dario believes it was the same poison. And that complicated how convinced he was that *you* killed my father."

"I didn't," he argued.

"I doubt it, because why would you use the same poison that was used on Luka? And I highly doubt you killed Luka because you were too busy with me at that time."

He grinned, moving his hands from my ass to shove my dress up my thighs. "I remember."

"And—"

Knocks sounded on the window, and we both flinched, turning to look out the windows. They were tinted. All these Mafia men drove in privacy like that.

Two Bernardi soldiers stood outside, likely curious and concerned that their new Mafia prince's car was still idle here.

"Shit." Talking with Renzo had taken longer than I anticipated, and I hated to go at all. "Cover for me."

"What? Wait—"

I scrambled off his lap, going for the opposite door. "Get out on that side and make an excuse. Cover for me while I slip away."

He scowled, adjusting his semi-erection in his pants.

"It's the least you can do for my sharing that intel with you, isn't it?" I snapped.

"I thought we were supposed to be enemies."

I rolled my eyes. "Yeah, me too."

"Not… partners."

Damn, that sounded too good to be true. To have a sexy, strong man like him to rely on, that would be a dream. "Co-conspirators," I amended.

He did as I requested, stepping out to address his men, and I went out the other door to run to the car I'd driven here.

Being seen with him wouldn't bode well, but as I got into my car, I wished I could be running to him, my supposed enemy, rather than hurrying away.

10

RENZO

Renzo

Before Luka married Cecilia and died at his wedding, I seldom went into the office at my house. Luka lived with Gio in the Bernardi mansion, but because I was the spare brother and always preferred to remain out of sight and out of mind, I had my own residence.

Nowadays, I was in that damn room constantly, dealing with what felt like nonstop supervision.

I need to delegate. Or I need to delegate more.

We had a whole organization to rely on, and I didn't understand why Luka was so deeply involved in so many things at once. Didn't he ever trust our Family and our men?

Or maybe he just liked to micromanage. I did not, and already, I was leaving the capos and leaders to handle the little shit I didn't want to get tied up with.

Like leading an orchestra. I didn't need to be hands-on like Luka was. And I bet letting the men see that I trusted them would boost morale.

Dean was too valuable to ever dismiss, though. I spoke with him late into the night now, trying to piece together more details.

He was older than Gio, just barely, and the old capo knew goddamn everything about everyone. Loyal to the bones, the man was a diligent, dedicated, and highly resourceful man to lean on. Luka liked him too, so when I stepped into Luka's position, Dean became *my* right-hand man like he'd been for Luka.

He paced from one end of the office to the other, shaking his head. "I'm telling you, there are no leads. Anywhere."

I pursed my lips, taking his word for it. He'd been on the case from the start.

"Did you confirm that Isabella was drugged, though?" I didn't doubt Giulia, but I had to check and learn all that I could. Dean had spent hours following up that angle, and I wasn't shocked that he nodded now.

"She was, but her tox screen reports were erased."

I narrowed my eyes at the thick paperweight on the corner of my desk, zoning out. "Why?"

"She's as vain as they come, high-maintenance in her looks and reputation."

Unlike her eldest daughter. Giulia dressed impeccably, fitting right in with the other women of our world, but she never flaunted it. She knew she looked good, or she should know it, and I assumed that she was simply too confident to have to flaunt it. I had yet to witness her being selfish and vain, but I'd be waiting a long time.

Isabella might have given birth to Giulia, but they were not the same. Not even similar.

"I'd wager that she didn't want anyone to know she'd been drugged or made vulnerable."

"Do you think whoever did it wanted to kill her but failed?" I asked.

He shook his head. "I considered that, but that wouldn't make sense. Luka was killed. Rocco too. Why screw up when they'd already done it successfully twice before? If they wanted her dead, she'd be dead." Slumping into a seat, he exhaled a long, tired breath. "I wonder if it's someone from inside."

"In the Acardi residence?" I didn't like the sound of that. What if someone targeted Giulia? Or her sisters? They were too young not to be innocent.

Fuck. I'm not supposed to care. Not like this.

"From what our spies reported, no one on the Acardi security team has pointed out where or how someone could have trespassed to drug them."

I huffed. "Well, I know firsthand how shitty the Acardi security force is there."

He furrowed his brow. "You do?"

Shit. I waved at him, dismissing that angle. I trusted him, but I didn't want to tell him that I'd snuck in there and ended up with Giulia. I kept her secret not only because she'd asked me to, but also because it was *our* secret. I didn't want to share her, or anything we'd done, with anyone else.

If word got out that I'd been with her at the wedding or in her room—*or in my car*—her purity would be challenged.

Dean stood, yawning and ready to go home for the night. "What I need to figure out is how they got the poison to the wedding. How that drug got into Luka's drink when so many people were around at the reception."

"Could Rocco have done it after all?" I asked, doubting it as I spoke. "He was near the table, near the drinks."

Dean shook his head. "I don't recall his being there for long."

Dammit, he wasn't. I knew Rocco wasn't hanging around the head table near Luka and Cecilia because I heard him outside with Isabella, looking for Giulia.

"What are you thinking? That he killed himself out of guilt?" Dean asked. "If so, why drug Isabella too?"

I shook my head, waving him off again. "Go on. Sleep on it. We'll figure it out somehow."

As I retired and dropped into bed an hour later, I wondered how and why my brother's death would connect with Giulia herself.

In the morning, I reported in at Gio's study, curious about what he wanted. I had my days filled now, and if he wanted to nag me about finding the killer, I really would punch him. Never before had I realized how impatient he was. But then again, I hadn't ever had to really be near him for long.

I nursed a coffee as I took a seat in his study and waited for him to get off the phone. Once he disconnected, he faced me sternly. "Where's Cecilia?"

I frowned. *At least he's changing up his demands.* "Was I supposed to find her?"

"Not necessarily. I want your input. Your thoughts. Where the fuck is she?"

I smirked. "Have you taken the most obvious step of asking Marcus where she is?"

He shook his head and then rubbed his chin. "No. It's a delicate matter."

I snorted. "Cecilia. She was delicate." Mousy and shy, intimidated by her shadow, it seemed. She was nothing like the bold, calculating woman that Giulia was.

Fuck. I've got to stop thinking about her. Since she snuck into my car, she'd been on my mind. We'd kissed, but surprisingly, the moment we shared wasn't an attempt to fuck or get her off.

Friends. That was what we'd behaved like. Something like friends, not enemies, and it showed me how valuable she was becoming to me.

"And I can't blame Cecilia for running and hiding somewhere." I shrugged. "She just got married, and at her wedding, her husband died. For someone with a weak disposition, I bet it would be traumatizing. Maybe she needs to accept her loss and all that."

"Well, I'll raise the matter with Marcus tomorrow. I'll be meeting him at the club, and I expect you to come as well."

"To talk with Nickolas?" I asked. He'd already mentioned it to me, and I hadn't forgotten.

"Yes. To discuss the drug trade arrangement he'd started to plan with Luka. It'll be a good first step to taking over that project."

Great. I nodded, masking my sarcasm and lack of enthusiasm. The last thing I wanted to do was sit down and have a conversation with that hotheaded asshole. I didn't look forward to listening to the prick who thought he could have any right to Giulia.

But who was I to judge or get mad?

She wasn't mine.

No matter how much I wanted her to be.

No matter how perfectly she seemed to fit and belong with me, not as a needy, clinging wife to order around and knock up.

But as a partner. A friend. As something more, and definitely something I never could have anticipated finding in my enemy.

As my other half.

11

GIULIA

Giulia

I wasn't sure if Renzo took my intel to heart. He had to believe me, that there was a connection between his brother's death and my father's. They'd died so close together and so similarly that it couldn't be a coincidence. I'd never really believed in those, anyway.

I lacked another chance to sneak away and meet up with him again.

Half of the urgency to see him was to check whether I was going crazy, if I was imagining this pull to want to be near him all the time. The other half of my wish to approach him was for answers.

I understood that he wanted to find Luka's killer. But now, it was irrevocably tied to me, too. Because if someone killed my father and attempted to murder my mother as a means of taking over the Acardi name, and me, I wanted to be prepared.

"I'm telling you," Uncle Dario insisted after I saw my sisters to bed. He sipped his drink in the library then shook his head. Bags lined under his eyes. Bloodshot and tired, he looked three times his age, and I felt terrible that he felt so stuck about our circumstances.

He couldn't be the head of our bloodline. After his injuries, he had to accept the fact that he'd never have children, and as such, the Acardi name would die out with him. I knew he was frustrated. I saw it every time he spoke with my father or mother about important matters. He'd been pushed back, delegated as a useless Family member, but right now, in this week after Father died, he'd been a sounding board for me.

Mother stayed in her room. She had been cleared and discharged from the hospital, but other than the watered down funeral for Father, she complained of headaches and needing to stay in bed.

Which left me with Uncle Dario to figure out how to move forward.

Except, he remained lodged at square one, refusing to reconsider who could've killed Father.

"Renzo Bernardi killed Rocco," he insisted.

"I don't agree." I crossed my arms.

He narrowed his eyes, tracking me as I paced. "Why?"

I glanced at him. "What do you mean, why?"

"He's no friend of yours."

I resisted a cringe. *False.*

"You don't know him."

Again, I fought the urge to show my feelings about that remark. *I want to know everything about him.* The little I'd been treated to so far rocked my world. He could both make me explode with pleasure *and* just be there and comfort me without any expectations in return.

"Neither do you," I shot back. "The only reason you're fixated on accusing him as Father's killer is because you overheard Giovanni Bernardi ask him to avenge Luka. He didn't tell him to specifically kill Father, did he?"

Uncle Dario smirked. "No." He knew he'd been jumping to conclusions and thinking he heard something that hadn't actually been said. "But they hate us. The Bernardis have always been our enemies and always will."

But why? No one would ever fucking explain why. "Because…?"

"I don't remember the details, and whatever bad blood happened in the past hardly matters." He glowered at the ceiling, as though he wished he could bore a hole through walls and scorch my mother in her room. "Because *she* will always make sure they remain enemies."

I considered his perspective. "Wait. Has my mother accused the Bernardis of killing Father and drugging her?" He'd talked with her the most since she came home from the hospital, bossing him around. She banned me from "bothering" her during her unnecessary bedrest.

But that doesn't make sense. The same drug was used on Luka, and that would have to imply that someone with the Bernardis wanted Luka dead.

"No. But she loathes them. Always has, for the 'principle' of it, as she says." He lowered his head into his hand and rubbed his face. "Let's say Renzo didn't kill Rocco."

I nodded.

"That fucker would still know something. Giovanni would too. Renzo's been seeking answers, determined to figure out who killed his brother. He's got to know something by now."

If he does, how would we know? He wouldn't dare sneak into the house again. Not after the uptick in security after Father's death and Mother's drugging incident.

"And I'm not sure I would trust what he says, anyway."

I would. I do. It happened quickly, but I knew that Renzo wasn't the enemy he should be. We were in this together, somehow, and I planned to consider him an ally until something or someone suggested I shouldn't.

"Which is why I think you should try to spy on him."

I blinked wide, staring at him. "*Me?*"

He nodded. "I received word that Renzo and Giovanni are meeting with the Romanos at the club."

I didn't need him to say which one. It was the neutral meeting grounds where all the Mafia men stopped to chat or see dancers. I'd found Renzo there, taking a chance that he might be there so I could tail him and hide and wait in his car.

"And…" I narrowed my eyes.

"Disguise yourself as a dancer." He glanced around as though he worried someone could overhear. "And spy on them. The Bernardis and Romanos. Get information, Giulia. We cannot continue with this cluelessness."

It sounded like a ridiculous plan, but as soon as I envisioned pulling this off, I was excited to take the risk. I wasn't sure I could be a covert spy, but I would use this as an opportunity to get close to Renzo and speak with him.

"You want me to spy on the Bernardis meeting with the Romanos?"

He nodded. "Just listen in. We need answers, and I don't know who else to trust to get them."

"I'll do it." I wasn't sure if I kept the excitement out of my reply, but I prepared to leave anyway. A former maid's daughter danced there, and once I arranged to meet up with her, she quickly got me into a costume and helped me figure out which of the private rooms Renzo might be in.

Suited in a revealing outfit and hiding behind a masquerade-like mask, I joined the other dancer who'd been requested to that private room. As I followed her, nervous and excited, I worried that I couldn't pull this off. Lap dances? Gyrating on men?

Whatever. I wasn't a prude. While I had to remain a virgin until marriage, I'd seen my fair share of porn and naughty videos. My mother insisted on giving me an in-depth lesson of sex education when I was fifteen—to prepare me for what would be expected, she'd claimed.

Still, when the doors opened and I joined the other dance in the room, nerves hit hard.

The lamps were set low, but the spotlights blinded me. They were directed to the area between the lounge chairs where the men sat, and I knew that was where I'd be expected to perform.

Following the lead of the other dancer, I mimicked her swaying and sinuous motions. It was all a glorified attempt to grind against the man while thrusting my breasts out. Nothing too complicated.

The second I spotted Renzo, though, I lost my confidence.

He stared at me, locked on my eyes, and I watched as he tensed. His hands sat on the armrests and he dug his fingers into the plush surface. As he clenched his jaw, he exhaled short, quick breaths, nostrils flaring, fury shining in his eyes.

He'd spotted me, all too quickly, and I knew the ruse was up.

Nickolas was oblivious, seated across the open space. While I was grateful it was just the two of them here, with the standard pair of bodyguards standing in the back, Renzo's presence threw me off.

I wanted to speak with him. I wanted to entice only him, but I was stuck in this role now.

Nickolas and Renzo carried on their conversation as I danced with the other woman, but after a while, their conversation dried up. Nickolas's leery focus was pulled from their chat about some drug business.

He stared at us dancing, and when he beckoned me closer with a curl of his finger, I did my best not to panic.

THE LAST VENDETTA

No. I quickly sidestepped, letting the other dancer mistake his summons and go to him.

"Wait. I want that one," Nickolas said, shaking his head at me as I backed up toward Renzo. Nickolas patted his lap and spread his legs out. Between his fingers, he held dollar bills. "Come on."

Renzo grabbed me. His fingers wrapped firmly around my wrist as he tugged me back, but I fell, startled and unbalanced on my feet.

"Yeah, help yourself to the clumsy one," Nickolas taunted. He grabbed the other dancer's hair and fisted it as he pushed her to the floor. "Suck me, bitch."

Renzo caught me, hauling me onto his lap. This close to him again, I was safe. Under his hold, even though he gripped me too tightly, likely furious, I was secure.

I was right where I wanted to belong, but the tic on his face revealed how tense he was.

"What the fuck are you doing?" he whispered into my ear as I danced on his lap, leaning back to his chest.

"I…" I couldn't speak. Nickolas might recognize my voice. It was a stupid worry. He wasn't paying attention to me or Renzo. As the woman took his cock into her mouth, he groaned and forced her head to bob over his length faster.

Would Renzo expect me to do the same? Here? Like this? I hadn't counted on having to get *this* physical. And while I wanted Renzo so badly, I didn't want to risk taking my mask off. Nickolas had already removed the other dancer's.

"I… I need to go." I didn't wait for permission. Scared of all the guards in here, and so near Nickolas, I succumbed to the churn of anxiety and fear in my gut.

Even though Nickolas seemed appeased, what if he turned to me next? What if—

No. Panic claimed me, and after I scrambled to my feet, stuck with the pressing feeling that I couldn't breathe fast enough, I ran out of the room.

Breathing hard, I shoved my hair away from my face and ran.

Pounding footsteps chased after me. I should've counted on it.

They all rushed after me, and I whimpered with terror as I sprinted.

Renzo was right on my heels, but behind him were the furious Romano guards. They must have alerted others, because another man ambushed me around the corner, holding me captive.

The two guards with Renzo were no longer there. Nor were the original two Romano guards who'd been in that private room.

Captured and pulled outside to an alley, I struggled and kicked to get free.

"Release her," Renzo ordered.

The metal door clanged shut, and the guard dropped me. I fell to the pavement roughly. My knees stung. My palms ached. But I stopped my fall before getting hurt any further. On my knees, I stared up at Renzo as he stood between me and the two Romano guards.

"What the fuck is going on?" one demanded.

"Is she a spy?" the other asked, pointing his gun at us.

Renzo wasn't slow on the uptake. He brought his gun out, aiming it right back at him. "Leave her to me."

"She's a fucking spy." The first, taller Romano, sneered. "Bringing extra backup to a confidential meeting with the Boss, huh?"

"She's not a spy," Renzo growled, countering the guards as they tried to approach me around him.

"Take off your mask, whore," the second one ordered.

"Just grab her," the other said, waving his gun to gesture for his partner to pull me off the ground.

I scrambled closer to Renzo, hiding behind him.

With my heart lodged in my throat, my side stitching with the need to breathe faster, I clung to Renzo and did my best not to pass out from the dizzying, nauseating hit of panic.

"Just—"

Renzo fired, hitting the guard who reached for me and yanked me by my hair.

"You motherfuck—" Another gunshot ended whatever the other Romano soldier would've tried to shout.

Renzo fired twice more, sinking bullets in their heads.

Then he turned to me, furious. His eyes glittered with rage as he lowered to haul me into his arms, then over his shoulder, and ran.

12

RENZO

Renzo

"**D**o not say a fucking word," I told Giulia as I set her on her feet and shoved her to get her into the car.

I sprinted around the vehicle and slid into the driver's seat. By the time I turned the car on and sped out of there, I had Dean on the line. Anchoring my phone between my ear and shoulder, I drove out of there as fast as I could.

Of all fucking women to show up *there*...

"I need you to clean up at the club." Ignoring Giulia's shallow, quick breaths from the passenger seat, I focused on driving as fast as I could and telling my right-hand man what I needed. Those Romanos in the alley would need to be disposed of. The cameras back there would need their footage wiped clean. And more men would need to be present at the club to explain to Nickolas why I'd disappeared.

Damage control. I dealt with it swiftly, knowing Dean would handle it all.

By the time I finished instructing him, I'd reached the underground door to the building Giovanni owned. It wasn't the fanciest building in the city, but it was a convenient stopover. Luka used to bring hostages to the basement. Other Bernardi men used it as a place to hide things. And on the top floor, I'd carved out my niche with a bachelor pad when I was too wasted or lazy to drive all the way home after partying.

I led Giulia up there. While she didn't protest, I didn't care for her searing glare. I felt her glower, her incensed stare as I forced her into my penthouse, but I didn't give a fuck if she thought I was being bossy.

"What the fuck were you thinking?" I demanded once I shut and locked the door.

She didn't cower. She didn't fidget. Standing tall in the middle of my living room, she lifted her chin. Defiant. Stubborn.

"What the *fuck*"—I gripped her chin and forced her head up so she'd look me in the eye as I stalked up into her space—"were you thinking?"

She stalled, pulling her lower lip between her teeth to worry the plump flesh.

"Answer me!" I released her and growled, so furious that I couldn't contain it.

Looking her over, I took in the full effect of her disheveled, slutty attire. The dancer's costume was ripped, torn and dirty from the fall to the pavement outside. Her long black locks hung over her shoulder, but on her other arm, the fingerprints of that fucker's grip remained visible on her skin.

Red and angry. Just like how I felt that another man had dared to touch her.

Seeing her in there had stunned me. I'd almost lost it as soon as I locked eyes with her, knowing without a doubt that it was Giulia in that sexy outfit, dancing in a private room at this club.

There was only one reason she'd ever try to sneak in as a dancer. One.

She'd come to spy. On me or Nickolas.

"Do you have any fucking idea how stupid that was? How dangerous it was?"

She crossed her arms, sassy and defensive as I roared at her, but I was too livid to let her think she could stand up to me like this right now.

I growled, stalking toward her. She lost her stance, lowering her arms and backpedaling.

"Spying on a fucking meeting?" I yelled as I went after her. She tripped, fumbling her way around the furniture and through the room, but she didn't dare look away.

"I need information."

"That you couldn't have fucking asked me for?"

She scowled, slamming her back against the door frame to my bedroom. "Oh, yeah, right. Cut the shit. I can't ask you for information."

"The hell you can't." I shoved her toward the bed, letting her climb back up to sit.

"Because we're great friends now, huh?"

I clenched my teeth, pinning her to the bed. "If you had to know something that goddamn badly, you could have fucking asked me."

She pressed her lips together tightly, staring up at me with hatred.

"Spying in there like that…" I growled and shook my head. "How fucking stupid are you? They would've recognized you and known you snuck in there."

"I had a mask on," she argued.

"So fucking what? I recognized you immediately."

"Because you know—"

I slitted my eyes. "Because I know you? Huh? But you thought you could sneak in there undetected?"

She looked away, turning her head on the bed, and I grabbed her chin again, pressing my body weight down on her until I got her attention. "Don't you know your fucking place?"

"Of course, I do! I'm just a supposedly stupid woman stuck in a vulnerable position while my Family falls apart. That asshole in there might want to make me his wife. His plaything, like he did that other dancer. And unless I can figure out who killed my father, I have no leverage to get out of anything like that!"

"You're crazy," I growled. "You're fucking insane."

She pushed her head up to yell louder. "I don't care! I don't care if you think I'm the stupidest woman on earth. All I wanted to do was figure out something—anything—that could explain why I'm facing marriage to that bastard."

"So, that's your answer. You think you can disguise yourself and spy and get ahead."

"I don't want to get ahead. I just want to avoid a worse fate than what I already have."

"They were going to kill you," I said, wishing I could shake sense into her. "They captured you, suspicious of why you ran out of that room."

"Because I was afraid," she shouted, likely hating to admit it. "I was afraid he'd turn to me next, take my mask off, and see that I was there." She sucked in a quick breath, riled up from fighting my hold and shouting.

"You should've been terrified." I leaned up, looking her over. Feeling her breasts rubbing against me threatened my determination to scold her. This skimpy dancer's outfit taunted me.

Caught between fury and desire, I lost the willpower to resist this urgency to teach her a lesson she'd never forget.

"If Nickolas knew you were spying…" I ground my teeth as she scowled at me.

He would've killed her. Raped her and tortured her, then slowly taken her life.

This bold, brave woman. One I couldn't imagine seeing gone.

"What the fuck were you trying to learn?"

"Anything," she snapped. "Anything. I need to know what the hell is going on. I have to figure out who killed my father."

"And listening in to me and Nickolas would've revealed that?" I grabbed her wrists in one hand, stopping her fighting. "How'd you know we would even be there?"

"My uncle."

"He—" I ground my teeth. "Dario fucking sent you there to spy?"

"On you," she sneered. "He still thinks you killed my father."

"You don't believe me?"

She narrowed her eyes. "I want to. And *that's* the only reason I'd be stupid. To want to believe you."

"So, after I killed those guards for you," I said, ripping her costume off, baring her completely. I grabbed the fabric to twine it around her hands. "After I saved your ass and got you out of there…" I unzipped and shoved my pants and boxers down. "And after I spared you from that sick fucker learning that you came to spy…"

I shoved her legs apart, hovering over her. Her pussy glistened, soaked with her arousal.

"This is the fucking thanks I get? Another accusation that I killed your father?" I slammed into her, sinking my cock in as far as it could go.

She arched back, groaning at the hard slide in. Even though she was slick, warm, and wet for my entrance, she'd never had a dick in her before. No one had ever impaled her like this.

"You think you can risk your life and be a spy," I growled as I pulled out of her tight cunt. "And had the right to say you think I killed your father when I told you I didn't?"

I slammed back in, watching her breasts jiggle with the force of my hips pounding against hers.

"Huh?" I grabbed her thighs, forcing them up. "That's the thanks you want to give me for saving your life and rescuing you?"

"Fuck you." She shook her head, breathing hard as tears streamed down her cheeks. "Fuck you, Renzo."

I groaned, riled up even more at the way she'd still try to piss me off and push her luck. I fucked her harder but slower, making sure she felt every ounce of fury as I stretched her virgin cunt.

"I…" She moaned, trying to move against me. With me. "I'm supposed to be clean."

A virgin. "Not anymore." I grinned, slamming into her sweet pussy. "This cunt's mine now."

She shook her head. "I'll never be yours."

I lowered until I hovered over her body. "You'd rather have Nickolas claim you, then, huh?"

She sobbed, crying harder.

"Because that's exactly what he would've done," I threatened as I filled her, over and over. "He'd take you and ruin you."

"Just like you are?" she demanded.

I stopped, staying still so deep inside her. Every pulse of her pussy spurred me to go faster and fuck her until I soaked her womb with my cum. Her breast rubbed against me, taunting me with her soft skin against my chest.

So small yet fierce, caught under me and wrapped around my dick.

She was perfect. And I wanted to keep her just like this.

"I didn't kill Rocco," I repeated.

"You didn't have to fuck me to emphasize it." She sniffled, staring up at me with glossy, angry eyes. "I didn't think you did. But my uncle doesn't know how to figure out what my family can do now. My father's dead. My mother's still messed up and in bed. Nothing is certain anymore."

I watched her, mesmerized by the sheen of tears in her eyes. It wasn't an act. Neither was the cream that dripped for me, the heat of her pussy sucking me in more.

"I'm desperate for answers."

I was too. I wanted to uncover the truth about who was poisoning members of the Mafia.

"But now it doesn't matter, does it?" She scowled at me, letting her hatred take over. "Now, I'm just damaged goods." With her hands still bound and above her head, she was without options to shove me off.

I doubted she would. As I stayed still inside her cunt, I felt the tension of her body. Slowly sliding my hand over the curve of her ass, I held her tighter. "You're welcome."

"Oh, fuck you, Renzo. I didn't want you to do this."

"No?" I grinned, pulling out and relishing the slow, throaty moan of need she couldn't keep in.

"I don't want—"

I thrust into her harder, stealing her breath. "No," I got out from my clenched teeth as I fucked her. She felt too good. I didn't want it to be over too soon, but I wouldn't last. "Your line is supposed to be *thank you, Renzo.*"

She growled, futilely pushing her hips up to match me thrust for thrust.

"You should tell me thanks for saving your life."

Her breasts bounced faster, and I wished I could delay her orgasm.

"You should be appreciative that I got you out of there."

A long, sexy groan left her lips as I sped up and ground over her clit.

"And you should say *yes, do what you want with me.*"

She tensed. All her muscles locked down as she neared her orgasm. As her face contorted into a grimace, I dug my fingers into her ass and drove in her wet heat even harder.

"Please," she begged on a frantic exhale. "Please, Renzo."

With the first wave of her pussy clenching my dick, I faltered. Her orgasm seemed to sweep through her, making her thighs tremble and her feet shake. And still, I kept at it, fucking her like my life depended on shattering her to pieces.

A short scream heralded her climax. Then with another hasty inhale, she cried out louder.

That was all it took. Hearing her come and lose to the bliss of the release, I followed right after her.

All those days and nights since I first touched her at the wedding had finally come to an end. Our epic buildup of need and desire exploded.

We'd crashed and burned, coming together in such a mind-blowing release that I wasn't sure which way was up any longer, where she began and I ended.

We were one now, fused through anger and joined with lust.

And I'd be damned if she tried to fight me on this connection ever again.

13

GIULIA

Giulia

Renzo's phone rang before he could pull his throbbing dick out of me. He groaned as he jerked inside me and his cum filled me.

I lay there, stunned by what happened.

He'd taken me, so roughly and suddenly, pushed to action by both fury and desire.

Renzo had fucked me without thinking, without asking me first.

I was no longer a virgin. I was claimed, and by a man who couldn't keep me.

He growled as he dropped his head to my shoulder. Breathing hard from the exertion of fucking me, he delayed in getting up and let the ringtone continue.

"That had better not be Gio." He pulled out of me quickly, and I hissed at the sting of slight pain. Standing next to the bed, he looked down at me with an unreadable expression on his face, almost as though he couldn't believe that he'd just fucked me.

"I don't know how Luka ever dealt with this shit. Always on. Always something to do, somebody wanting something." He rubbed his hand over his face, standing tall and proud.

Naked, with his dick shiny from our cum. A hint of red showed on his penis too.

My blood. My virginal blood.

Ten minutes ago, he'd wanted me. He'd finally acted on this rabid sexual tension that snapped between us. It was a small consolation, to know now that he'd been suffering from the same damn need that I'd struggled to deny and hold off.

Shock from his actions returned, chasing away the bliss of the orgasm. Seeing him just as bewildered proved that he hadn't really planned this either.

How could he have? I surprised him by showing up as a dancer at that club. He hadn't planned on finding me there to premeditate bringing me here and raping me. In the process of teaching me a lesson and scolding me about the sheer stupidity of spying at that club, he'd lost the fight to the never-ending attraction that still burned between us.

I loathed him. He'd taken my virginity. It was done now, but I still couldn't help but cling to the satisfaction of how good it had felt in the end.

"I don't need to make every fucking decision for everyone to feel important," he groused, grabbing his phone from his pocket in the pants on the floor. "I don't need to be bothered constantly for every little fucking thing."

It sounded like he wasn't acclimating well to being Giovanni's second in command.

But that hardly mattered right now.

With another deep sigh, he shook his head and headed out of the room with his phone. "I'll be right back," he said.

I won't. He seemed annoyed with this call, like he needed more time to figure out what to do with me. I wasn't sure what my next move should be—except to get the fuck out of here.

He left me to take his call, and as soon as he was gone, in the bathroom suite, I scrambled out of bed. Ignoring the burn between my legs, I wiped the small trace of blood on his sheets and grabbed his clothes. My teeth helped with the knot around my wrists. The dancer costume I'd borrowed was a mangled scrap now, and in order to get out of his place, I'd need real clothes.

His shirt and pants draped over me, but they would keep me decent. Before he could return, I rushed to the door and undid the locks.

No guards stood outside the door, and while it seemed odd, I bet it was another detail that Renzo struggled with. As the heir, the next in line for the Bernardi Family, Renzo had to have a security detail to protect him.

Not that he can't handle that himself, I mused as I ran out of his apartment.

He hadn't hesitated to chase after me and save me from those Romano guards who'd been so suspicious of me at the club. He hadn't thought twice about saving me from those men.

I was grateful. I owed him my life. But to pay him back with my virginity?

Not now. I couldn't let my emotions control me at this moment. I'd analyze it all later, when I was safe at home and able to get over the shock of all that happened tonight.

My clothes were still at the club, where I'd been dropped off. My phone was at home. Dario agreed with me that preventing any tracking would be smartest. Instead of worrying that I was stuck without a way to go home, I headed to the nearest cover business my Family owned and operated to launder money. The restaurant was a seedy little hole in the wall, but from there, I could call home and ask Dario to send me a ride.

Only once I was in the backseat of the hired car did I fully exhale and let out all the tension I'd bottled in. The night had begun with such a simple goal. My uncle asked me to spy to get information. I'd obtained none. And lost my virginity in the process.

My God...

I covered my face with my hands, closing my eyes and trying to shove back the reactions I didn't have time for right now.

I couldn't believe I'd done it.

Renzo hadn't given me much choice, but I didn't exactly resist him, either.

Because I'd wanted him too. And I refused to feel guilty for taking what I wanted. For the first time in my life, I'd gone for what I desired, and nothing could shame me into regretting it.

My sisters were still asleep when I arrived, and as soon as I finished changing into my own clothes and hiding Renzo's in my room, I went to find my uncle in the library.

"Giulia." He looked up with such a bright expression of hope that I hated having to report in at all.

I shook my head and carefully sat on the couch across from him.

"What happened?"

Renzo Bernardi fucked me. "Nothing." I cleared my throat.

"What? What do you mean? Weren't Bernardi and Romano meeting at the club?"

His stern tone held authority that I couldn't ignore. Despite his handicaps from his injury, Dario was still a hard-edged Acardi man. Had he not been wounded when I was just a child, he'd be the spare brother, the younger brother to Father. If he were "whole" and not weak and unable to bear children, things would be so different.

The Family wouldn't be falling apart with Father dead. Dario would have simply stepped up and done well. He was the one who taught me to pick locks. He was the relative who didn't go out of his way to dismiss me as a stupid girl.

If things were different, he would've been in charge now. Just like Renzo had to adjust to taking Luka's place.

"They were there," I replied, choosing my words carefully. "But they only talked about a drug trade. Nothing about Luka, nothing about Father." I frowned. "Nothing about me, either."

He sighed but then sharpened his gaze. "What do you mean? Why would they talk about you?"

"Did Father approach the Romanos about arranging a marriage between me and Nickolas?"

He scoffed. "No!"

"You're not aware of that?"

He shook his head. "Hell no. Rocco wouldn't have been that stupid. With Cecilia marrying Luka and Nickolas to marry you, Marcus Romano would control the next two most powerful Families."

A monopoly.

He was so quick to catch up. Uncle Dario had a lesser role in the Family, but he didn't miss anything. Shrewd.

"Did you kill Father?"

He rolled his eyes. "No. Why would I have? What would that do? For power?"

I shrugged, feeling like I was grasping at straws to make sure he didn't ask too much about what happened tonight.

"Would you support arranging a marriage for me now that Father is dead?"

"No."

"But we have no stability. No man to lead the Family. No sons who would soon lead."

He shook his head. "Absolutely not. I can't speak for Isabella. She's been acting sick in bed all week, but I've heard her on the phone when I pass her room. She'd better not be arranging you in anything. That's the only leverage we have to use. Your remaining unattached and unclaimed is the only power we have to prevent the Acardi name from being owned by someone else."

Too late. It's far too late for that.

I was attached. I had been unofficially claimed in the truest sense of that word.

Renzo had. He'd taken me.

"And we need to keep it that way, Giulia."

I nodded.

"Until all of this settles. Until we have a better idea of who is an ally and who is our enemy."

It still won't matter. I had sex with the enemy. He'd owned me sexually, but I knew he wouldn't be so stupid as to announce it. He wouldn't want to risk Giovanni's wrath by suggesting he align our Families together now.

It was a fluke moment. A perfect one, now that I could sit and think back to the feeling of him stretching me and pushing me past the pain to experience so much pleasure.

I wished Renzo could keep me forever. To repeat that bliss. To show me more. He was rough and controlling, but at the end of it all, I hated to admit that I'd enjoyed it. I reveled in it, and I felt terrible to want it again.

I'd never counted on having any power, no right to choose my lover or man.

But now that the deed was done, I couldn't deny the deep, twisted sense of pride and satisfaction in knowing that Renzo was the one to take my virginity.

No one else.

14

RENZO

Renzo

I wasn't surprised that Giulia left after I fucked her. She hadn't exactly been expecting it. Neither was I.

I got caught in the heat of the moment and it just… happened. But I didn't regret it. I lay in bed all night wishing she could have stayed, but I understood that she'd had to bolt. To hide. To get over the shock that we'd given in to each other in the most physical sense possible.

The morning after, I met with Gio in his office. Nursing another coffee, waiting for the caffeine to kick in and wake me up all the way, I watched as he tried to finish up with a phone call. Just as I was coming to learn, we were always in high demand. I didn't think that I had to be on call constantly, but I would figure out a balance. It was early days yet.

I had to get a better grip on my time. Because I would be damned if I'd have another beautiful, sensual woman in my bed and have to be interrupted by a phone call about something that I didn't really care about.

Luka had wanted to be in control of everything. I wasn't like that. Delegation was key, and if someone proved themselves untrustworthy without my hovering over them, then they would be dead. Simple as that.

Gio disconnected the call and faced me. Since Luka died, Gio seemed to consider me in a new light. Half the time, he seemed bothered, like he couldn't believe that his esteemed firstborn was gone. And the other half of the time, he seemed almost amused, as though he doubted I could ever step into my brother's role or stay on top of as much as I had so far.

"Why did you take off from the club last night?" he asked as a greeting.

After Giulia left, I stayed home and tried to think through what I could do with her now.

She was the reason I'd left the club like I did, then had to deal with damage control for killing those guards. I wouldn't mention her. I couldn't. I didn't return to the club because I hadn't wanted to.

"We talked about the drug trade," I replied. And that was expected.

What wasn't expected was how different Giulia would be now. She was no longer the same. I stole her virginity and I wouldn't apologize for it, but I had to contend with this deep, burning jealousy and possessiveness that I couldn't shake.

I'd had her once. And I was now addicted to her, wanting her again.

I was stupid enough to wish I could have her forever.

But I couldn't tell Gio that, either. It was bad that he somehow knew I'd taken off so abruptly from the club, but there was no way I'd share the whole truth with him.

"Before the conversation came to a close, I got a call about something I had to deal with."

He nodded. "That's how this business works. Never a moment of peace."

That was bullshit. What was the point of having power and wealth if we couldn't ever stop to enjoy it for a single moment? I felt a unique and deep peace when I came inside Giulia, and I knew that would never happen again.

"Did everything go well with your discussion with Nickolas?" he asked.

"Yeah. It did. It seemed like Luka and Nickolas had smoothed out all the details already."

"Good." He folded his hands together on his desk. "I also had a productive conversation with Marcus."

That had been the plan. I went there to speak with Nickolas while he met with Marcus in another private room.

"About what?"

He stared at me for a long moment. "We discussed Cecilia."

"Does he know where she is?"

He pursed his lips. "I think he might not. I didn't come out and ask him that, specifically. We more or less spoke about what should happen to her now."

I didn't give a shit about what happened to my sister-in-law. It wasn't as though I knew her. I'd be damned if they expected me to get involved.

"I proposed a potential situation to him, that she should just marry you now."

Fuck. So much for not getting involved.

"Me? Why?"

"Marcus remained tight-lipped about where she might be. He wouldn't directly admit it, but I got the impression that he didn't know where she was and he wanted her to come home where he could control her. Where he could watch and see what she was up to."

"And how the fuck would I play into that?"

He narrowed his eyes. "Don't get that attitude with me."

"I don't have an 'attitude'." This was simply my blunt and honest reaction. *Why me?* The thought of marrying that boring, quiet woman seemed like a death sentence.

"Listen here. If I tell you to marry her, you will."

"Like hell." I stood, leaving my empty coffee cup on the table. "You actually put this into plans last night with him? Marcus is on board with this?"

He sighed. "No, not yet. Not officially. We were merely discussing ideas."

"Then I don't have anything to worry about."

"Don't act like you have any control here. Do not even think about having any right to say yes or no to anything I arrange for you."

"Because it's just another part of business," I mocked. "Right?"

"It is. And we would be wise to align with the Romanos. I attempted that with Luka marrying her."

His phrasing made me pause. "Do you think somebody killed Luka because they wanted an alliance with the Romanos instead of us having one?'

"Marcus spoke about that quite a bit. But he's a shady asshole who never gives anything away."

That was the truth. The Romanos were wealthy and had an old influence that couldn't be contested. But they were sneaky cheats, too.

"I left with the impression that Cecilia won't let her father know where she is. Marcus brought her up first, almost leaning on the idea of your marrying her to root out whether I knew anything about where she was."

I wondered if Giulia would know. Isabella had been gossiping at Luka's funeral.

Maybe I could ask Giulia to listen for more news. She'd report to me. She did willingly of her own accord when she made the connection between how Luka and Rocco died. It was just one of the many things about her that I admired. She could have kept that fact to herself, the similarity of the poisonings, but she'd openly shared it with me.

As soon as this thought about Giulia came, I tried to ignore it. I couldn't be going on like this, acting like that sassy, smart woman was my ally. My friend.

My partner.

But it was all too easy to see her in that light. She was intelligent. Quick. Observant. If she didn't know where Cecilia was hiding, she would have ideas about the woman's motivations.

Why would Cecilia kill Luka, though?

Unless Cecilia was traumatized or too sensitive after losing her husband… Why run away and hide at all?

Luka had been killed at the wedding, and the timing of it stood out to me. Why not kill him before? Or later? I didn't understand why Luka had been killed when he was.

Maybe the killer could only reach him in that big crowd? It warranted more thought.

If someone wanted to avoid a Bernardi-Romano union, they would've had to kill him before they shared their vows. The only likely enemy who'd want to stop the Romanos from aligning with us would have been the Acardis.

Maybe Rocco did kill Luca. And he killed himself afterward from the guilt and to escape justice.

That didn't seem likely, though.

Could Cecilia have done it?

I considered the possibility of Luka's timid, short-term wife killing him. Cecilia hadn't been enthusiastic about marrying him, but no arranged couples were excited about their chosen partners.

Like Giulia. She dreaded the possibility of marrying Nickolas. I hated the thought of his having her too. It killed me that he'd seen her dancing last night. If I had any say in it, that fucker didn't deserve a second of being in her presence.

Is Cecilia hiding out of guilt? She killed Luca and needs to lie low? But why?

If she hadn't wanted to marry him, it would've made more sense to kill him before the wedding.

As I left the house after my talk with my father, I tried to figure out how I could reach Giulia and speak with her about this. I felt stuck in my head, both with the way she wouldn't get out of my mind and with all these speculations that led nowhere. She'd have opinions. She'd be able to tell me what she thought of my guesses.

I no longer saw her as my enemy. I couldn't when I was desperate to check on her and make sure she was all right after last night. She'd been so tight, so young and innocent, and I knew I'd taken her harder than she might have wished for her first time. My efforts were too late. But wasn't it the thought that counted?

If she wasn't my enemy, I couldn't label her as some ordinary easy pussy, either. She wasn't an average nobody I'd fucked on a whim.

Giulia was coming to be a true friend. Someone I instinctively knew I could count on.

She was…

An equal. A brilliant, brave woman I would be proud to call my own. And once again, I wished I could make that happen, to freely go to her whenever I wanted, for whatever reason.

Or even without one. I wanted access to her for good, for the hell of it. Because when she was near, when she welcomed me to touch her and drive her to the brink of an intense orgasm, I felt more alive than I'd ever been. And when she simply listened to me and shared ideas or intel, I felt like I wasn't alone or struggling but one half of a true pair where one could always depend on the other.

15

GIULIA

Giulia

The morning after Renzo took me to his place, I woke up groggy and disoriented from poor sleep. All night long, I suffered flashbacks of the memories that would live forever in my mind.

The rub of his muscled arms against my sides. The clutch of his fingers on my ass. The pulling cinch of that fabric around my wrists, disabling me from freeing my hands.

"Stop," I groaned lightly to myself as I got out of bed. "Stop thinking about him."

It was impossible. Because as I started a scalding hot shower to massage my body, I couldn't turn off the phantom reminders of how he felt.

Over me. In me. Everywhere. The desire he'd stoked in me coursed through me with a feral intensity, and I didn't think I'd ever feel normal again.

Was this simply what it felt like to no longer be a virgin?

Or is it because it was him?

I stepped into the stall and hoped the hot water would massage me and render me awake.

Last night, I showered and cleaned off the stickiness of our cum and the little bit of blood, but today, as I let the water soothe my rattled mind, I felt depressed. That was it.

Once.

I'd enjoyed the harsh perfection of Renzo deep inside me one time, and that was all I could ever hope for. His Family loathed mine, and what remained of my Family wasn't any better. Dario still seemed to suspect Renzo killed Father. Mother hated all the Bernardis. Trying to look forward to a repeat of that unexpected passion was a waste of time.

I eventually left the shower, my skin numb and raw, and I knew this uneasiness and sense of longing would have to fade.

Downstairs, I found my mother seated in a chair in the summer room.

I stopped short, almost spilling the coffee I'd just made.

She sat there, calm and collected as she sipped her coffee, and my suspicions grew immediately.

What is she *doing here?*

Since Father died, she'd been holed up in her room. Francis claimed to have overheard her speaking on the phone, but I hadn't seen or spoken to her since the rushed excuse of a funeral she'd ordered to hold for Father.

If she was grieving, fine. I wouldn't have believed she cared that he was gone. She'd never shown him an ounce of love but made sure to consistently harass and nag him when he was alive.

If she was still sick from whatever drug she'd been poisoned with, she didn't make any requests for medical assistance.

Seeing her was a shock. I saw no hint of an emotional or physical weakness. She looked as normal as ever, face taut and unexpressive, even bored.

But why was she *here*?

This was where I always took my coffee. She hated it, claiming the plants looked tacky and the tinkling sound of the ornamental waterfall from the sculpted water pool in the corner of the sunny room was annoying.

She was deliberately seated in *my* place. Coupled with her sudden reappearance, she seemed to be up to something.

"Morning," I said cautiously, coming out to sit next to her.

I wasn't stupid. She had to have chosen this spot to force me to speak with her. I seldom had to deal with her in the mornings. Like my father had, she preferred to keep her personal time a priority over being a present mother.

She lifted her gaze to me, studying me. It was stupid, but I couldn't help the worry that she was looking *through* me. As though she could know what I'd done last night. She wouldn't have approved of Uncle Dario's suggestion that I spy for intel about Father's death. And she definitely wouldn't like that Renzo had fucked me.

"What's wrong with you?" she asked for a greeting.

Shit. I wasn't any good at hiding it. I wasn't doing anything out of the ordinary, but just hearing her suspicious tone set me further on edge.

"Nothing." I set my coffee down on the table too quickly. I didn't need to add caffeine to my already frazzled status. Without another word, I headed for the exit to the gardens outside.

She wasn't going to let me off the hook. Waiting for me in the place I always sat and drank my coffee was only her first plan. As she hurried after me, the glass door swung back, almost smacking her in the face. It still didn't stop her.

"Giulia."

I shook my head, not in the mood for any of her games. I'd never trusted her, and I wouldn't start now.

"What do you want?"

"To talk."

I narrowed my eyes at her as she rounded me. Standing on the path, she blocked me from walking off. "About what? Father?"

She kept her lips pressed in a tight line.

"You've holed yourself up in your room for over a week." I crossed my arms, letting my natural loathing for her conceal how unsettled I'd felt since Renzo took my virginity.

How absurd. I could trust him, the enemy, but my mother provoked me to be defensive.

"I've had to handle all the condolences. I've had to ward off all the questions about why we didn't even really hold a funeral for him."

She shrugged. "That doesn't matter."

I slitted my eyes further. "Why? Why did you choose such a pathetic funeral? Are you trying to ignore the fact that he died?"

"Ignore? No one can ignore that he's dead."

I shook my head, letting all my pent-up confusion and anger come to the surface. "Then why are *you* ignoring it? You rushed for a private funeral. You won't speak to anyone. You hide in your room and—" I groaned, already exhausted from dealing with her at all.

"I was grieving."

I smirked at her. "Really? That's the line you're going with?"

She raised her brows. "I was grieving."

"You never *cared* about him to grieve him."

Tilting her head to the side, she seemed to almost smile. Like I was amusing her. "And you did?"

I gawked, stunned that she'd be so... cavalier about this. "Are you trying to say *I've* been acting unusual about his death?"

"Your father's death is something none of us can change."

What? Obviously, we couldn't. He wouldn't be coming back from the dead. While her cool wording suggested that she'd come to terms with losing him, she seemed too indifferent. I didn't expect my mother to be sad, and she didn't look one bit upset. But she was taking this way too calmly.

"However," she added, causing another twist of dread to knot my stomach, "his death does necessitate our making changes for the future."

I stared at her, nervous and worried. This heartless woman was always scheming. Always planning. And her goals were always to secure her own best interests, no one else's.

"Such as?" I lowered my arms, then crossed them again because I needed the comfort of something like a hug. Whatever she would have to say would be bad news. I just knew it.

"You will marry Nickolas Romano."

Her words were a death knell.

I knew it. Renzo had put the idea—the fear—in my mind. He'd mentioned overhearing Nickolas talking about marrying me now that Father was out of the way.

So many frantic questions filled me as I stared at her.

Did Father not want me to marry Nickolas? Could he have killed him because of that rejection? And what, did my mother want me to marry him and she could go ahead with those plans now?

"Why?"

She smirked, like I was being petulant and silly. "What do you mean, *why*? Why else?"

I shook my head, refusing to look at her and just accept this punishment.

"We need to secure an alliance with the Romano influence. To gain the support of their wealth and strengthen our Family now that your father is dead."

"Not like that." I thought back to Renzo's accurate description of her. She'd need to heel. She would have to listen to the Romanos. She'd no longer be able to nag and scold the people who controlled the money.

"It's not your choice to make."

I glared at her. "Nor is it yours."

"Oh?"

She was the widow of the former head of the Family, but until all the will stipulations were seen to, she was no more powerful—as a woman—than I was at the moment.

Reminding her of her insignificance in our world wouldn't change anything. Instead, I tried a different counter. "Uncle Dario thinks that avoiding any marriage arrangements would be smart. At least until we know who killed Father."

"Dario?" She snorted and rolled her eyes. "He's not the leader. He's not the Boss of this Family."

"But he's Father's brother, the de facto man in the Family whom any marital arrangements should come to for *his* consideration."

"Dario is weak," she spat.

"He's sound of mind," I argued. "And he's willing to stand in until we know who our enemies truly are."

"I *know* who our enemies are." She stepped closer, trying to intimidate me but falling short. Literally falling short. I had two inches on her and I wouldn't be kowtowed.

"Don't be stupid and think that you have an opportunity or freedom to make your own choices. You have no power in your future."

"Nor. Do. You."

She lifted her hand to slap me, but I deflected it. Before Dario was injured, he and Francis taught me more than the basics of self-defense.

"You should know your fucking place, Giulia." She flung her arm back, seething.

"I do know my place."

"Then shut up about this. You won't get out of this arrangement. You *will* marry Nickolas and spare me from ever having to put up with your impertinence ever again."

What about my sisters?

What about Dario?

What about... me?

"He's a monster," I told her. Trying to win her sympathy wouldn't work. She'd made up her twisted mind, but I had to speak up.

"They're all monsters. Monsters or weak fools, like your father was."

I shook my head. No. "Nickolas isn't someone I can marry."

"It's not a matter of whether you can. You will."

"He's…" I panicked, swallowing down the whining sound that clawed at my throat. Too many memories filed through my mind. All those rumors and stories. "He's a sadistic asshole."

She huffed.

"All that stuff about that whore," I reminded her.

"Luka was with that woman when she died. I heard it was suicide, anyway."

"Because of how Nickolas tortured her!"

Was this her way of saying she didn't care if *I* died after staying with Nickolas?

"Then I suppose you should try to prepare yourself now for what's coming."

How can you be so cruel? So heartless and unloving?

"You should know by now that no man who is fit to be your husband will be a soft, pathetic gentleman. That's not the way this world works. So get your mind off the thought of a ridiculous fairytale ending."

"I don't want a fairytale. I want to live without fearing my husband!"

Over her shoulder, I caught a glimpse of Renzo sneaking through the hedges. I should've been shocked that he was trespassing—again. That man knew no bounds to taking risks where I was concerned. But seeing him here meant he'd overheard this death sentence.

Exactly what he'd tried to give me a warning about.

"Don't be such a child," Mother scolded. "You're going to marry Nickolas and spread your legs for him to bear him a child. Whether you want to or not."

My lungs seized. I couldn't breathe. The mere thought of enduring anything from Nickolas pushed me toward a colossal breakdown.

Never.

Renzo was forceful with me. But I enjoyed it. I felt so full and alive under his forbidden touch, and I yearned for him again. Despite the punishing attitude he'd had when he pushed me to the bed, I knew he'd been doing it with affection.

It would be the opposite with Nickolas.

And I vowed not to find out.

Back by a tall length of hedges, Renzo hid in the shadows.

There was no way he hadn't overheard it all. Besides, he'd already known about the possibility of this union from whatever Nickolas had said.

I had to see him. I had to talk to him. Just being near him would soothe the throbbing agony in my head at the mere thought of being forced onto Nickolas.

I didn't know why he was here, but I assumed it was to see me, too.

"Is this all that you wanted to tell me?" I demanded of her, eager to be out of her presence and away from whatever she was plotting.

She dragged her wicked gaze over me, looking for something else to bitch about. "For now." Instead of letting me tell her to get lost, she turned and headed inside.

Remaining where I was, letting her think that she'd had the last word, I waited for a long moment. Zoning out at the manicured grass, I stalled until she'd entered the house and was gone from the windows overlooking the garden.

I glanced up, catching sight of Renzo at once. A slight tip of my chin indicated for him to head toward the side where my room was.

If he'd climbed down the trellis near my balcony, he could climb back up it, too.

LEONA WHITE

He nodded, and I spun around to run to my room and wait for him.

16

RENZO

Renzo

Meeting Giulia in this clandestine manner wasn't smart, but nothing could keep me away from her. Seeing her reaction to Isabella's mandate that she marry Nickolas was difficult. I saw how she'd flinched, as though she were hit. I bit my lip and stayed hidden when the mother tried to slap her for insubordination. As she grew quiet and pensive, I worried she was sinking into a pit of despair.

Fuck, Giulia. You can't marry that bastard.

I disliked the idea of her marrying anyone, but I knew that was a ridiculous sentiment to hang on to. Of course, she'd need to marry someone sooner or later. I simply hated that it could be *him*.

I climbed back up into her room, glad for the weeping willow branches that surrounded her end of the mansion. It made it easier for me to scale the trellis then reach for her balcony.

She was waiting there, frantic and impatient. Grabbing my hands, she tugged me inside her room. Then once she'd closed and locked the glass doors, she guided me into her bathroom.

"What are you doing?"

The shower ran, but no steam collected.

"I can't risk anyone hearing us," she explained. The running-water trick was an old one, but it would mask our conversation if anyone lurked in the hallway.

"And now that she's over her 'mourning' period and no longer wants the world to believe she's 'recovering', I can't trust that she wouldn't be out there snooping." She locked the door as I leaned against the vanity.

Seeing her so calculating yet worked up made me want to go to her and hold her close. I admired her foresight to disguise that I was here. I enjoyed how seamlessly she wanted to confide in me. And I hated that she was upset about this at all.

What the fuck is happening here?

It was bad to care, but now I was letting myself get in deeper.

For the wrong woman.

"That…" She clenched her teeth, pacing. "That bitch!"

"She's being hasty," I commented. "I just overheard Nickolas in passing that day, and now she's communicating with him about it."

She nodded, glancing at me with heat in her eyes. "Yeah. I know. And I bet she was working everything behind the scenes all that time she was hiding in her room."

Probably.

Meanwhile, I was busy fucking her daughter.

"She's being too hasty. And it's never good to rush into things like this. I know my father's death came unexpectedly for her, but this hurry to shove me into a situation with Nickolas isn't going to solve anything." She pointed at me. "It's like you said. She won't want to be under someone else's control and have to wait for permission from a more powerful man. She could harass my father all she wanted, but she can't do that to Nickolas or Marcus Romano."

"Then why does she really want you to be aligned with them?" I crossed my arms, thinking about what Gio had said.

"Power. Wealth." She shrugged but looked at me closely. "What are you thinking?"

"Something Gio mentioned." I looked her dead in the eye. "That someone might have killed Luka to foil his plans of having the Romano connection. Could Isabella be thinking that very thing?"

She frowned. "To cheat the Bernardis out of the Romano alliance?" A bitter huff followed her words. "I could definitely see that. She's never made it a secret that she loathes your Family."

I narrowed my eyes. "Why?"

"Why would she make it public knowledge that she loathes your Family? Because she does everything like that. Loud and unhappily. And wanting to spread the misery."

"No. Why do the Acardis hate us? Why have we been raised to think of each other as the enemy?"

Finally, she paused in her pacing to face me. The troubled expression on her gorgeous features suggested that I had her there—confused and without an answer.

"I don't know." She arched a brow. "Do you?"

I shook my head. "No. Just what I was always told."

"Same."

"But…" I rubbed my hand over the back of my neck. "The lines are blurring."

"They blurred. Past tense." She pointed a finger at me and hardened into a scowl. "*Only* once." Slipping back into pacing, she covered her face with both hands. "You took my virginity, Renzo."

I intercepted her, hugging her tightly. "Don't wait for an apology."

She growled lightly and shook her head. "I'm… I'm not asking for one."

"Fuck. Don't do this." I lowered my head to hers, kissing along her jaw. "Don't—"

"I don't regret it," she argued, turning to press her lips to mine. My dick hardened, and I struggled to breathe past the instant hit of desire that overcame me. Before I could deepen the contact and taste her smart mouth, she pulled back and evaded my touch.

"But I do know it can't happen again." She laughed once, mirthlessly. "We cannot have sex again. Not when I'm promised to that monster."

The frustration and longing in her voice cut at my heart, but I heeded her wishes. Staying back by the vanity, I watched her pace faster.

"He's terrible. I don't even want to know what you could tell me about him. I've heard enough rumors. I can't…" She shook her head. "I won't marry him."

I admired her strength and determination. But there was no way out of this. She had no voice.

"Uncle Dario almost laughed at me when I asked if he knew about any plans for me to marry Nickolas. He said no. He thinks we should wait to arrange any marriage until we have a better idea of who our enemies are."

I nodded. "I agree with that."

"I'm not asking for your opinion." She softened the bite of her words by glancing at me. "And you can't do anything about it either."

"I already have. You're not a virgin any longer."

She groaned. "Yeah, but we can't be together due to the rivalry. Shit! What if Nickolas is furious that I'm not clean?"

"Don't say it like that." I knew damn well what she meant. Unclean as in no longer a virgin. I disliked the suggestion that my cum didn't belong in her. It did.

"What if he takes it out on me when he realizes I'm not a virgin?" she asked, her dark eyes so wide open with vulnerability.

"I don't think..." I licked my lips and lowered my gaze. The weight of her direct focus was too much to bear. I hadn't thought about that last night. I'd been too overwhelmed with the need to fill her. Once I saw the evidence of how badly she'd wanted me too, my control snapped.

"What?" She wasn't letting me off the hook easily. "You weren't thinking last night."

"Neither of us were." I narrowed my eyes. "Like sneaking into that club and spying."

She groaned.

"I don't think Nickolas will necessarily know you're not a virgin."

Her lips pressed tightly together. Her nostrils flared. She was *not* happy with my input, and I was so damn fallen that all I could think was how gorgeous she looked like this. Mad and passionate, smart and doing her best not to be hysterical about her predicament.

"They don't always check for blood, and..."

"And he'll rape me so hard and quick, he won't even realize anything else."

I winced. *This can't happen.*

"She's unhinged. Crazy. I mean... To expect any of her daughters to be with Nickolas?" She shuddered.

"This is how it works," I reminded her.

"I *know* that." Again, she rubbed her face. "That's how things work in this world. But if I run…"

What? I pushed off the vanity to approach her. "No."

She stared at me, deadpan. "So you think I should just grin and bear it?"

"No. But running?" I shook my head. I couldn't stand to think of her gone. She could stay, be my mistress and avoid her husband as much as she could. I couldn't choose my bride any more than she could choose her husband, but we could still be able to meet up.

"There has to be another option out of this."

"Like what?"

"I don't know." Her deep gaze captured me. "But with Luka's death, then my father's so soon after… I can't stop thinking that something bigger is at play. And whatever it is, this new shakeup of power and enemies and secret plots, I want nothing to do with it."

"Running away isn't the answer."

She rolled her eyes. "I know that."

"I doubt it could even work." If she jilted Nickolas, he'd run after her, bring her back, and make her pay.

"Then, what else is there to do? No one will confess to killing Luka."

She narrowed her eyes. "You don't have any ideas?"

I shook my head. I did, but nothing she wanted to hear. This was a serious conversation about a heavy topic, but my control was still so thin. Being alone with her tempted me.

"What'd you sneak over here for, anyway?"

I took her hand, pulling her close. "First, I wanted to see if you were okay."

She huffed and yanked her fingers away. "Because of last night? Yes. Against my better judgment, I'd do it all over again."

"But I also wanted your input about Cecilia."

Perking up, curious, she cocked her head to the side. "Cecilia Romano?"

"Yes. She's missing. And my father was wondering what's going on with her."

"Because she's his daughter-in-law?"

More like he's determined to make her an active daughter-in-law.

"Yes, but Marcus seems to not know where she is either, and he wants her home where he can control her."

Her smile was sarcastic and sad. "See? I'm not the only woman who wants to run away and hide in this world."

Don't. Please.

Because Giulia was the only woman I wanted to keep close, however I could.

She was the one person I didn't want to flee and hide away from everyone.

Unless she was doing so with me.

"You don't have any ideas about where she might be?"

She shook her head.

"You haven't heard any gossip?"

The sassy smirk she gave me taunted me to desire her even more. "The last time I tried to get intel and eavesdrop didn't turn out so well."

I scowled. "No, it didn't."

"I haven't heard anything about Cecilia."

"Not even from Isabella?"

"Nope." She shook her head. "Until this morning, when she wanted to explain that I was engaged to the devil, she'd been in her room. I haven't spoken with her all week. Even at the 'funeral' for my father. She didn't speak to any of us."

With that account, it would've been easy to assume that the woman was suffering from immense grief. The only catch with that was how horribly she'd treated Rocco. Never with love, and very public and vocal with her disgust and annoyance with him.

"That doesn't mean she won't have a clue," Giulia added. "I think she was in her room planning and living in peace just fine."

"I won't ask you to speak with her, but…" I raised my brows.

She shrugged. "I'll see if I can eavesdrop or something. Someone's got to know something."

I nodded.

Sooner or later, the truth would come out. But even after it did, I wasn't sure it would help anything between me and this amazing woman I wanted to call my own forever.

"We'll figure something out." It was a weak promise, but I had to give her some indication that I didn't want to leave her stranded with no options.

"Oh, yeah? How?"

"I don't know. I'll think about it. And we'll… figure something out."

"Something that would avoid my having to marry Nickolas?"

I grimaced.

"I will run, Renzo. I cannot be with him. Not after I could see how good it is with you…" She shook her head and headed toward the shower to turn the water off. Pressing a kiss to my cheek was the only detour she allowed before stepping out of my reach again. "I know better than to hope for a repeat or any future for us, but I know that my fate will not be tied with him."

17

GIULIA

Giulia

After Renzo left, I let the idea of running away sink in fully.

Could I do it?

All I'd ever known was this Mafia life. I was born and raised under the expectations of being a pawn to be married off. I grew up without having any goals for myself because there never would have been a point to carving out my own purpose. Everything was dictated, and until Mother told me that I would be expected to become Nickolas's wife, I'd done my best to tolerate this existence. To just get through it, day by day. Being a support system for my younger sisters filled a hole in my heart. For them, I could smile and be the dutiful elder daughter I was expected to be.

But as I lay in bed that night, I came to the honest conclusion that I could not do this.

I couldn't marry that man, not under any circumstances or self-sacrifices.

I wasn't sure if it was because I knew what and who I wanted. Renzo. I yearned for him even though he was off-limits as my Family's enemy. And I missed his touch, even though he was rough and took liberties that shouldn't have been his to begin with.

Knowing how much I wanted Renzo turned me off from being able to surrender to Nickolas.

But I wasn't sure what other options I could follow.

If I ran, how would I bring my sisters along? I would never abandon them. I couldn't.

And how could I plan to stay away and hidden? I had wealth. I was sure Uncle Dario would help me access it somehow. My uncle had always seemed to care about my well-being more than Father had. I *knew* Mother didn't care about me at all. She couldn't if she was considering marrying me off to Nickolas Romano, of all people.

She was the one I wasn't sure how to escape. If I ran, she'd track me down. If I tried to leave this confining life, she'd hunt me and do everything she could to get me right back where she wanted me.

But Cecilia did it.

I stuck with that thought. Cecilia was out there hiding somewhere. If I had to guess, she simply wanted peace and privacy to get over the trauma of Luka being killed at their wedding. That was a horrendous event to recover from. I doubted she cared about him. Like me, she was just another daughter to be brokered like an item. She couldn't have loved him, but she did have a gentle, skittish demeanor.

I recalled the screams she let out at finding her husband slumping over, dead. While violence and death were staples of this Mafia life, she likely had been sheltered from witnessing it up close and personal like that.

If a newlywed wanted to break away and rest in privacy for a while, I supposed she had an excuse.

But if she was trying to run, if she was trying to shed this identity of a Mafia wife...

How'd she pull it off?

Maybe she could give me pointers.

The next morning, I woke with that same current of determination that I'd fallen asleep to. If Cecilia could run and hide, then I damn well could try to as well. If she could take off after Luka's wedding and do so without her father knowing where she was, that was saying something. Marcus Romano was wealthier than my Family, and if someone could deceive him, that meant she was *really* lying low.

After I tended to my sisters, checking that they were fine with their tutors, I felt better about checking that task off my to-do list. With our chaotic and unstable family structure, I wanted to make sure I wasn't slacking in being present in their lives. They were too young, still innocent, and I wanted to keep it that way for as long as I could.

Because no one ever did that for me.

I was nine years older than Marianna, but that gap of siblings wasn't intended. Mother tried constantly to get pregnant after she had me, but it just wasn't feasible. When she grew convinced that her difficult labor with me had rendered her infertile, she held a grudge against me, sometimes never even seeing me and letting the team of nannies make sure I was alive and well. Then when she miscarried a couple of times, she blamed Father for her inability to give him a baby. She never, ever let herself believe it was her fault. It was mine. Or his. Science was a finicky thing. Fertility and conception weren't to be faulted to any one person, but she'd warped us all to never mention the chance that *she* was the reason they didn't have more children sooner.

What made it infinitely worse was that all her pregnancies, both viable and not, were all daughters. Men ruled this world, and Mother only worsened her attitude and treatment of us when she failed to not only get pregnant and confirm that she carried a son, but also in her inability to never give Father an heir.

And if I become Nickolas's wife, I'll be expected to give him a son.

I placed my hand over my stomach, fighting back the worry that Renzo could have knocked me up the other night. He hadn't used protection. It hadn't even crossed my mind, so mad, scared, and aroused all at once.

If I were carrying Renzo's son, a Bernardi heir…

No. Just don't even think about it.

I would definitely have to run far and fast if he'd impregnated me. Yet, the idea of having Renzo's child didn't sicken me. It didn't bother me. If I allowed myself to really think about it, I felt… triumphant. Happy. My so-called enemy was the sort of hard man who'd take care of his own, and now that I'd had a few glimpses of the softie he could be beneath the hard surface, I felt even closer to the risk of falling in love with him.

Francis met me in the solarium like I'd requested last night. Before I went to bed, I sought out the loyal guard and asked him to look into Cecilia's whereabouts. He had connections. I had no doubt all these guards did. Just like the Mafia lords and ladies maintained their circle of acquaintances, I was sure the soldiers, capos, and guards did, even across enemy lines.

I considered asking Uncle Dario, but then I worried that would somehow implicate him. This "investigation" that Renzo and I had teamed up on was a secret, private partnership, and asking Francis for help was a safer option than asking Uncle Dario.

The less chance I took of someone being suspicious about my looking for Cecilia, the better.

"Did you find anything?" I asked once I closed the doors behind me. Francis had beaten me to the solarium. He stood near the back windows, gazing out at the horticultural sculptures out back. Always alert, always watching. In a little way, I knew I'd miss him once I left. He was a familiar source of security, or he was supposed to represent it.

"I did." He faced me, checking that we were alone. "But if I may…?"

I waved my hand, gesturing for him to go ahead. "You know you can always speak your mind with me, Francis."

His lips almost lifted in a smile. "Yes."

"I'm not my mother," I reminded him snarkily.

"Indeed, you are not." He cleared his throat. "If I may be so bold to ask, why do you want to know where Miss Romano is?"

I licked my lips. I couldn't tell him that Renzo and I were trying to be sleuths together. That was my secret.

"She is my peer."

He arched his brows. "And potential sister-in-law?"

I clamped my lips shut.

"Miss Giulia," he began carefully.

"I don't want to discuss my future."

He sighed and nodded. "Should you ever need my help, though—"

I huffed. "Help?" I raised my brows. "I wouldn't need help dealing with my fiancé." I would need assistance getting away from him.

"If you should attempt an alternative solution for your future…"

Now it was my turn to fail at hiding a smile.

"Then please know that I have *your* best interests in mind. Politics will never change. But I've seen you grow from a sweet child into a generous and kind woman. You have my allegiance."

I broke all protocol to hug him. It was a risk, but after the tumultuous ups and downs, I couldn't help it.

"Thank you."

He patted my back before we parted. "Now. Miss Romano."

I nodded. It was back to business. "Have you learned anything?"

"Yes. She is residing at the villa up along the coast. One of her family's vacation properties."

"Residing? Or hiding?" There had to be a difference. If Renzo was correct in saying that Marcus didn't know where his daughter was, her choice of a location made no sense. It wouldn't be that hard for him to find her there. Or any number of employees could tell Marcus where she was.

Unless Marcus is trying to act like he doesn't know where she is...

"I cannot tell. My sources only confirmed that she's been there since Luka Bernardi's death."

"Your source?"

He nodded. "A member of the Romano security detail." Then he handed over a small slip of paper with an address on it.

"Thank you, Francis."

Now that I knew where to find her, I'd go and get some damn answers. I couldn't be sure what Cecilia could tell me that would help me figure out who my truest enemies were, but it was a start.

"Should I arrange for transportation?"

I grinned, appreciating how well this man truly knew me and understood that I wasn't just another docile, ignorant woman. I really appreciated that he was loyal to me, not my mother, and would keep the secret of anything I was planning to do.

"No, thank you." *I'll figure it out.* I would ask Renzo to come with me. It only seemed right since we were both mutually curious and working on this together.

"Is there anything else I can do for you?"

He'd already done so much. But now that he was here, another question struck me.

"What started the rivalry between the Acardi and Bernardi names?"

He furrowed his brow, seeming stunned by that question. It was out of the blue like that, but I felt confident that he'd have a guess. He was older than Father had been. Francis came on as a guard when my grandfather ruled.

"I'm not certain," he admitted. "But I think it had something to do with Arianna."

I blinked. "Arianna?" *Renzo's mother?*

He nodded. "Arianna Bernardi."

Biting my lip, I dreaded the worst. "Did... my father sleep with her?"

He immediately shook his head. "No. No, no. I don't think so. Arianna was quite besotted with Giovanni. From what I observed, she was very much a woman in love with only her husband."

Then... I winced. "Did Mother sleep with Giovanni?" Affairs were the first thing to come to mind with rivalries. Infidelity and honor. Those were the primary reasons Families engaged in rivalries.

"I don't know," Francis admitted slowly, rubbing his jaw. "But if I can be honest, your mother has always been too calculating."

"Tell me something I don't know," I quipped.

"She's too calculating in everything she does, and if there were one person to suspect of causing trouble between the Families, I would think of her."

THE LAST VENDETTA

Francis received a summons on his ear piece, and that ended our secret chat. I thanked him again, and as soon as I left the solarium, I went to my room and called Renzo.

"Hello?" he answered, likely suspicious of the unidentified number.

"Can you talk?" I asked.

"Call me back in a few minutes."

I wasn't worried about his reply. He was likely near someone who could overhear. Or he had to deactivate the tracking on his phone. I gave it five minutes and called again.

"How did you get my number?" he said for a greeting.

"I have my ways." I'd found it in my father's office after the funeral. "I know where she is."

"You do?" He huffed a laugh. "You work quickly."

A smile lifted my lips. *He* lifted my spirits.

"Considering you shouldn't be 'working' at all, especially not like this."

I rolled my eyes. "Sorry, not sorry. You should know by now that I'm not a pushover like the other women in our lives."

"Where is she?"

"I'll show you."

He grunted. "What?"

"I want to speak with her."

"To bond with your future sister-in-law?"

I grimaced. *Not happening.*

"Are you coming?"

"Giulia. Listen to yourself. You can't just go and act like a soldier or operative. You—"

"Do *not* give me the illusion that you actually are just like every other man in my life."

He growled. "Let me handle this."

"No. Are you coming with me, or not?"

"That's what partners do, isn't it?"

I bit my lip, smiling again. Partners. I wished we could be paired for life.

"I shouldn't be partnering with you at all," he admitted. Just that simple admission cheered me. I heard every note of longing in his words. He knew better than to seek my company, but he was just as beholden to me as I was to him.

"But there's no way in hell I'll sit back and let you wander off like this without me."

It wasn't *I love you*, but it proved that he cared.

18

RENZO

Renzo

When Giulia called, she caught me off-guard. I couldn't risk the capo listening in while we dealt with a traitor, so I stepped outside. I wasn't sure that I had to be there personally, anyway. Luka used to supervise fucking everything. It was taking time for me to retrain everyone in the organization that I didn't need to be right there and watching over their every move.

If he said that the man had to be punished and killed for his incidents of lying, then I believed him.

At her word, I planned to leave. Traveling used to be a routine for me. Before I had to assume so much responsibility, I could do whatever I wanted, and I enjoyed taking off and going wherever I pleased.

Heading out of town with Giulia was the first chance I had to leave the city. I looked forward to it—both the opportunity to get away and the time I would have to share with her alone.

We were asking for trouble. Ever since the night Luka was killed, we struggled with resisting each other. Already, we'd lost so much ground in that fight. I made her come. We kissed. She came on my dick and milked me so perfectly. The other day, when we both knew better, we succumbed to kissing again.

Keeping my hands and mouth off her was an epic struggle. Hearing her admit how much she'd liked fucking me only goaded me to want her even more.

So, heading up along the coast with her was nothing but flirting with temptation. But it wasn't enough to keep me away from her.

I picked her up, as planned, at a seedy restaurant her Family owned. She was waiting in more casual clothes than what I'd ever seen her wear, and the laidback look suited her. I had no doubt her short black skirt was designer, as was the white blouse that accentuated the large swells of her breasts. But she looked looser. Calmer.

The smirking smile she gave me as I pulled up to the curb hit me square in the chest. She was radiant. Gorgeous. Full of life and excitement. And I reveled in the fact that simply seeing me coming for her made her grin like that.

Careful. I couldn't afford to fall any further for her when we were doomed to sink into a pit of hopelessness.

If Isabella was already making official plans for her to be with Nickolas, time was running out.

But maybe today will change all of that. A big reason I wanted to seek out Cecilia was to gain information about Luka's death, and probably Rocco's as well since it seemed that the same person had killed them both.

If Giulia and I could uncover who was killing these prominent men, there was a chance that Isabella might change her mind about foisting Giulia onto Nickolas. The Romanos were always shady as fuck. While an alliance with them suggested more wealth, at what cost would Isabella want them tied to her name?

I drove away, feeling more confident and in control with Giulia in the passenger seat. She didn't speak until we were further from the city. Once she opened her mouth to say something, my phone cut her off.

"What do—"

I growled at the ringtone. "I hate that thing." I answered, though, too duty-bound to think twice.

"Where the hell are you going?" Gio asked as a greeting.

I rolled my eyes. "Out of town," I replied.

"The fuck you are," he replied.

I glanced at Giulia, who raised her brows at the speaker call.

"Dean said you were taking off for some personal time," Gio said.

"I am." It was a personal matter to be with Giulia, even if we were working on finding Luka's killer.

"You don't have personal time anymore," he argued. "You can't take off and act like you don't have any responsibilities anymore."

"I can. And I will. I don't need to micromanage everything like Luka did."

"He didn't micromanage anything. He led our Family. He oversaw the men."

"And I can do the same while letting them actually do what is expected of them." I shook my head. "I'm not discussing this. You told me to step up and replace Luka. I am. I don't use the same supervision methods as he did."

"Oh, sure. I'm supposed to just trust you, huh?"

"Yes." *Because I'm your fucking son, remember?*

"You've never given me a reason to trust you so freely before."

"You also never gave me a chance to prove myself before." I didn't want to get into this with Giulia listening. I wasn't worried about confidentiality. I simply preferred to focus on anything other than Gio. "Since Luka's death, I've seen to every goddamn thing you tasked me with. Talk to me when I fuck up and you have proof of this incompetence you think I'm prone to."

I hung up, no longer in the mood to let him ruin another moment with Giulia. It wasn't like I could take her on a date or be seen with her in any romantic sense. I'd be in trouble if I were caught near her in the capacity of friendship, too. If going out of town to seek a woman who was potentially hiding was all I could use as a reason to get away with her, then I wanted to embrace every second of it.

"Hasn't been easy, huh?" she asked. "Stepping up to do what Luka did?"

I shook my head and rubbed my hand over my face. "No."

"I bet not. Uncle Dario was the same as you. The spare younger brother. But when he was injured and rendered unable to have children…" She shrugged. "I think in a way, he was relieved to escape all that duty."

Yet, her uncle was involved in the wake of Rocco Acardi's death. He'd sent Giulia on a harebrained mission to spy for information. It made me wonder whether he knew she was seeking out Cecilia now.

"I don't mind the duty. I grew up knowing I was the backup."

"Were you ever close with Luka or your father?"

I shook my head. "Not at all. Gio focused on him and has only ever paid attention to me when I had to step up. Gio is a businessman through and through."

"Unlike my father. He delegated as much as he could, much to my mother's distaste. She likes power, wielding it and hoarding it. She always wanted to know who was where and what power was at play."

I nodded. "That sounds about right."

She huffed.

"Gio told me the same thing. She's too calculating."

"She definitely is." As she turned to face me fully, I strained to keep my eyes on the road.

"Has she ever tried to calculate something with you? With your Family?"

I shot her a dubious look. "Like what?"

"I don't know. I was asking my guard about the rivalry between our Families. It's like we said. We were raised to know the other is the enemy." She flicked her finger back and forth between us. "But we never knew why."

"Lots of Families don't get along in our world." While the Bernardi name was a rival of the Acardi's, others operated around and beneath us. If any one of the patriarchs slipped and lost power, another would swoop in and take it for themselves. Or arrange a coup. Or stage turf wars to conquer more. It was a never-ending game of movable pieces and ulterior motives.

"He seemed to think that it had to do with our parents not getting along."

I glanced at her again, smirking. "I wouldn't be surprised. But it makes it more ironic that you and I…"

She huffed, shaking her head. "There is no *you and I*. We're co-conspirators in going to talk to Cecilia. I want to know who killed my father, and that ties into your wanting to know who killed your brother."

I took her hand and held it tightly. Instead of pushing away, she twined her fingers with mine, belying what she said.

"What about this pull to each other?"

"It's just physical." She swallowed hard and looked out the window.

It was physical. A visceral, gnawing need to touch and be close. But I was starting to suspect that it might be more than that.

"Speak for yourself."

She sighed. "Renzo. Don't. *Please*."

I ground my teeth, pulling over on the highway to slam the car into park. She gasped at the sudden stop, and with her caught unaware, I lunged over to kiss her.

Hard.

She parted her lips as I sealed my mouth over hers, and just like every other time, a sweeping wave of desire lit me on fire. Cupping the back of her head, I kept her close so I could devour her. It'd been far too long since I'd had a sample of her sassy taste, of earning her sexy mewls and feeling her tongue duel with mine.

"The only time I want to hear you say *please* is when you beg me to fuck you again."

She moaned, tipping her face up for a longer, deeper kiss. As she threaded her fingers through my hair, I shivered at the scrape of her nails on my scalp. If she kept this up, we'd both be a shaking mess of need.

"But we can't," she argued weakly as she twisted in her seat to crawl closer.

"Do you really think it's possible to tell ourselves no?"

She kissed me again and again as she grappled with her seatbelt buckle. I guided her, welcoming her into my embrace as she crawled over to sit in my lap. It was a tight fit, snug with her straddling me. Behind her, the steering wheel trapped her flush against my chest. Within my arms, I fought the nagging thought in the back of my mind that warned this wasn't wise.

I didn't understand how something so forbidden, something so wrong, could feel so damn right and good.

As she made out with me, moaning into our kisses, she clung to me like she feared ever letting go.

"You can't be with him," I insisted.

She shook her head, out of breath as I cupped her face to stare into her eyes.

"I know." She licked her lips, torturing me. "But I can't be with you, either. My mother—Gio—they'd never allow it."

I couldn't refute that, and kissing her silenced my need to reply.

"I won't be with him," she whispered as she rubbed over me.

I held her ass, urging her to grind over my erection, and kissed along the sweet flesh of her neck.

"I'll run. Whatever I need to do to avoid a life with him."

I dug my fingers in her cheeks, gripping her tighter as though I could hold on and prevent her from disappearing in the flesh.

"Because I only want you, Renzo." Her breath hitched as she kissed me soundly. "All I want, now and forever, is the enemy I can't have."

Fuck. She was killing me here. She spoke the truth, but I never wished for a lie more than I did at that moment. I wanted it to be false. I longed for a way to stay with her.

"Don't run," I told her. "Because I need—"

Gunshots rang out in the distance. Then closer.

She gasped, falling against my chest. I didn't wait. Hearing bullets hitting the car threw me into action. I held her tightly and turned her back into her seat, lowering her with my shove.

One glance in the mirrors showed me that men had found us. My instincts had been right. Someone had been tailing us out of the city. I'd lost them, weaving around and throwing them off our tail, but parked here for a stolen moment with Giulia made us vulnerable, sitting ducks.

Their cars were marked as the enemy. Not the Romano, Bernardi, or Acardi outfits, but another. The Greeks. I'd been so focused on Giulia and our conversation that I hadn't noticed we'd been driving near their territory.

"Stay down," I ordered her.

She was already slinking low in her seat, aware of what was necessary. No hysterics. No fear. Just the simple understanding of how things worked in our violent lives.

"Here." She handed me the gun from the glove compartment, competent and knowing what came next.

I took it, keeping one hand on the wheel. "You know how to shoot?"

She rolled her eyes at me, already sliding a smaller gun out of her purse. "Why wouldn't I?"

I laughed. If I hadn't fallen in love with her already, this cemented the fact that I would soon. "Because you're not a soldier."

"My uncle thought I should know a thing or two about defense," she quipped as she watched the side mirror, prepared to help me shoot our way out of the trouble on our tail.

19

GIULIA

Giulia

Renzo sped up to lose the Greeks closing in on us. When they failed, he counted on their colliding and getting in an accident to slow them down.

With deft maneuvering, he avoided crashing. But it wasn't enough. He slowed to fire at the closest car, and that did the trick.

I watched with my heart trapped in my throat, my pulse skyrocketing and my breaths so quick, as he shot at the front wheels. The SUV swerved, then flipped, and with the second car right behind it, that vehicle was smashed.

Large flames shot to the sky, but we were too far to be caught in the heat. Renzo kept a steady hand on the wheel and sped further away. Seeing him so tense and taut, his muscles flexed as he gripped the wheel and his gun, proved that he was no damn spare. He wasn't an inferior brother only now expected to perform as the Bernardis' second in command.

This wasn't the action of a man just suddenly coming into his strength or finesse as a ruthless Mafia man. He'd always been like this, always prepared to kill and defend, but I didn't know if it was himself or me that he was keeping alive.

"Are they targeting you?" I asked once several quiet moments filled the car as he sped away.

"Maybe you." He glanced at me, checking over me quickly. "Word spread that Rocco's dead. I wouldn't put it past them to try to take out more of your Family."

Which would make sense why Mother was drugged too. But no security footage showed anyone coming inside the house that night.

I nodded. "Or they want to attack with the knowledge that I'm Nickolas's bride."

He growled. "Don't fucking say that."

I sighed, trying to come down from the adrenaline rush and relax. We were safe. We'd gotten away, and knowing how much Renzo hated to hear of me as Nickolas's bride soothed my needy soul—needy for him.

"They could try to take me out to counter the Acardis aligning with the Romanos." It needed to be said despite how cold it sounded.

"I thought the same thing about Luka." He glanced at me, taking my hand and looking at me again as though he was still worried I could've been injured or stressed from that scare.

"You thought what?" I asked, holding on tightly. I had no right to seek comfort from his touch, but it was impossible to resist.

"That someone might have wanted to stop the Bernardi name from aligning with the Romanos."

I shook my head. "But that would have only worked if they'd killed Luka *before* the wedding."

He sighed. "I know. Which is why it doesn't make sense. And if that was the motive, *your* Family would stand to act on that motivation."

"My father didn't kill Luka."

"I know."

And he did. I could tell he hated to admit it, but the timing didn't add up. My parents had been outside looking for me when the poison had to have been slipped in Luka's drink. I'd considered the possibility of the poison being administered in his drink sooner, but it seemed unlikely. With all the drinks being ordered and given out, the killer would've had to ensure it was going *only* to Luka to get the desired result.

Before we could discuss it any further, my phone rang. I debated picking up when I saw it was my mother, but she would only continue to call me.

She was the enemy now, and it seemed prudent to keep an eye on her, keeping my enemies close and all. Once I spoke with her, I'd block her number.

"Hello?" I answered on speaker. If Renzo trusted me enough to let me listen in to a call with his father, I could return the courtesy.

"What the hell are you doing?"

I didn't reply. I stared at the phone, waiting for her to tell me what she knew. If she had a reason to call and ask me that, she had to be aware that I was, in fact, up to something. I'd disabled the tracking on my phone, so for all she could guess, I was in my room at home.

"I just received word that the Ornos Family reported casualties in a fight where *you* were spotted."

I rolled my eyes and slumped back in my seat. The flames from those burning cars would've been impossible to miss. Renzo's speeding car would've been noticed too. We'd been made, and I couldn't be mad about the fact. It was inevitable in any high-speed race.

"What do you want?"

"With Renzo Bernardi? That's who they suspect you're with. Are you fucking insane?"

Renzo's fingers tightened on the steering wheel.

"What the hell are you thinking?"

"What do you want?" I repeated. I wouldn't confirm nor deny that I was with him.

"I want to know what the hell you think you're doing."

"I don't owe you answers."

"Oh, you don't?" she sassed back.

"This is the last time I'll ask. What do you want?"

"So long as you are the unmarried eldest daughter of the Acardi Family, you will answer to me. You will listen to what I say."

I pulled my lower lip between my teeth, not replying. She always caved to the silent treatment. Always.

"Are you running away? Are you?"

"No." *Not yet.*

"Really. Because that's what it looks like to *me*. Are you running away with a Bernardi, of all people?"

"No," I repeated. I wished I could. The idea of taking off with Renzo—for good—sounded like a dream coming true. He didn't want to use me. He only wanted to show me how good it felt with him when we caved to the pressure of this sizzling attraction that bonded us.

"Think again, Giulia," she warned. "That's what people are going to say, that you're running away with Renzo Bernardi because you don't want to marry who I arranged for you."

I looked at Renzo, and he squeezed my hand. That simple touch comforted me more than he would ever know.

"You do understand that you're risking the wrath of Marcus Romano, right?" She huffed. "Not only are you trying to renege on the arrangement to marry Nickolas, but you are also interfering with Renzo's engagement to Cecilia."

My heart dropped. I blinked, trying not to fall into this zoned-out shock. *Renzo and Cecilia? Since when?*

An instant spike of pain lanced through me at the thought of another obstacle standing between me and this infuriating and stubborn man.

"He's arranged to be with her," she said. "I've seen to it that you will marry Nickolas first, but be aware of what you are doing, Giulia."

I had *no* clue what I was doing anymore. With Renzo, it was easy. I followed my heart. I obeyed this desire. Until I knew who killed my father and what was at play in the bigger picture of my world, I didn't know what was what.

"Come home. Now, Giulia."

"No." I couldn't censor my reply. I blurted it without thinking.

"You must. You come home right now."

"No."

She growled. "No? You have no right to tell me *no*."

After a week of her hiding in her room after Father's death, she was issuing her command with tenfold intensity.

"If you don't turn around and come home now, I will send a capo out to retrieve you. Come home, or let our men bring you home."

I shook my head and pressed the icon to end the call.

"Giulia—"

I sniffled, fighting back the tears that rushed to my eyes. "How could you keep this from me?" Wiggling my fingers loose, I tried to sever his touch.

He wasn't having that. Turning sharply, he pulled off the road again. I barely had time to brace myself from hitting the dashboard with his abrupt braking.

"I didn't," he argued, snatching my hand back again. He put the car into park and turned to face me. The severe concern shining in his eyes arrested me. The desperation in his tone persuaded me to listen.

"This is news to me."

I shook my head. "Don't act like I'm stupid, Renzo."

"You're not. Which is why it's so fucking infuriating to even think about being with a timid idiot like Cecilia. *You* are the intelligent, brave woman I want in my life." He slid his hand along my jaw, cupping my face. "I wish I could be arranged to marry *you*. Only you."

I swallowed, so moved by his risk to voice those sentiments. I felt the same about him, praying and wishing that he and I could be paired up. We meshed. We worked. If not for the stupid rivalry between our Families, we were a perfect fit.

"Giovanni mentioned the possibility of my marrying Cecilia."

"In other words, it was planned," I scoffed, still too guarded to be swooning and duped by his former words of something like love.

"No. I asked directly." He shook his head. "I asked if he'd set it into action and if I was officially arranged to marry her. He said they'd merely mentioned it. As a possibility."

"Well." I licked my lips and lowered my gaze.

He tipped my chin up, forcing me to maintain eye contact with his blue stare.

"It seems that something has changed, then. If my mother can say that with such authority—"

"Authority?" He grunted. "She doesn't have any fucking authority. No woman in our world has authority. She's got to be talking about rumors, using it as a way to convince you to run home where she can try to control you and force you to be with Nickolas."

I furrowed my brow, hating that he might have a point there. She very well could be using it as a tactic to sway me.

"But she said it. She wanted me to marry Nickolas before you could marry Cecilia. And in that case, you'd win."

His scowl preceded his heated argument. "*Win?*"

"The Romanos. This... competition to marry into their Family."

He exhaled long and hard. "I won't," he swore. "I don't want Cecilia, Giulia. I want you. I don't want to win the Romanos over. I don't fucking care what it could mean. I want you."

"That will never happen. Too many people would stop us from forming an alliance."

"Too late." He squeezed my fingers and leaned in closer. "We *are* allies. We're working together already."

I blinked, overwhelmed with this familiar warmth of desire that he stoked whenever he neared me.

"I want *you*." He sealed it with a tender kiss.

My heart sang with joy at his promise and sweet touch, but I couldn't lower my defenses.

"We'll go speak with Cecilia," he said. "I'll tell her that we won't marry. Ever. And if she doesn't have any information for us that will enable us to figure out who could've killed my brother or your father, then we will continue to work together—however we can—until a future that unites us is more possible."

I nodded then sighed, praying that he could be right.

20

RENZO

Renzo

What the fuck am I saying?

Two weeks ago, I could've promised Giulia the world. Back then, when I was still the spare brother, the useless one, I could've planned to fuck and marry whoever I wanted. Giulia still would've been a hard one to win over because we were enemies, but I wouldn't have been confined to these new duties as the second in command of the Bernardi name.

I was acting like I still had any say in my future. In my life.

But the hell with these rules.

If I wanted Giulia, I'd convince Gio to get over his goddamn rivalry with the Acardis.

She favored me, not Isabella.

She was running to me with information, not her mother.

She was choosing me in everything she did, and that led me to believe that if I fought for her, if I told Gio that she would be my bride, I had to have a better outcome and more hope than her telling Isabella that she wouldn't marry Nickolas.

As a man, I would have more power.

So it was with great impatience that I sped the rest of the way to the vacation villa where Cecilia was staying.

I wanted to see the damn woman in person and flat-out tell her that we would never be arranged to marry. Period. Full stop.

And the sooner I could personally deliver a hard rejection to Cecilia—and also show Giulia how committed I was becoming to her—the sooner we could start a plan for being together for real, for good.

I parked at the Romano property and immediately grew suspicious.

Giulia was as well, narrowing her eyes as she scanned the long drive empty of cars. "Where are all the guards?"

I shrugged. Of course, she'd noticed. This brilliant, beautiful woman was observant to a fault. She likely always had been because like all the women in our circle, she was dismissed to the background in our world. Unlike the others, though, she wanted to do something about her fate.

"Maybe Marcus decided not to have many guards here," she guessed as she reached for the door handle.

"To better keep her hidden?" I joined her outside, holding her hand and making sure she stood behind me as we walked up the path.

"Yeah," she replied, looking around and scoping out the area like I did.

Together, we approached the looming mansion. No one stirred. Nothing jumped out at us. The lack of activity and noise was disconcerting. Even if Cecilia was here to hide, some sort of staff should be present.

Giulia tightened her fingers on my hand. She caught herself from gasping too loudly, but she'd noticed it first.

"The door."

It remained open. Slightly ajar, the front door was left unattended. Unlocked.

I moved to shield Giulia from the doorway, more on guard and suspicious of this unusual setting. Cecilia was still the only daughter Marcus Romano had. She would need to be guarded no matter what, in marriage or not.

Giulia and I were the exceptions. We'd both run out on our own to keep our goals secretive, but it wasn't the norm. With the positions we held, it was expected to always have security with us. The same applied to Cecilia.

On edge, we entered together. I kept my gun up and trained, prepared to kill to defend myself and Giulia.

The first guard was dead, shot multiple times.

Shit. I hadn't counted on coming here to find a massacre. We might have arrived too late. If Cecilia was dead, there went our chances to get an answer today.

"Over there," Giulia whispered, showing me the other guard, also shot dead. He lay sprawled in the hallway to our left.

I nodded, paying attention to where we walked in the silent house.

Or not so silent.

A low groan came from ahead.

Giulia and I shared a look, and we hurried forward to find Cecilia.

She lay on the floor, a puddle of blood pooling around her.

Even though we were here together, I had a last-minute second thought about having Giulia reveal herself. Until we could know who

LEONA WHITE

was friend or foe, I didn't want to complicate anything for Giulia being here. If Cecilia could attest that she saw me with her brother's intended, she could spoil our surprise too soon.

I meant it. I wanted Giulia for good. But I had to plan to make that happen accordingly.

She didn't protest when I pushed her hand and indicated for her to wait in the alcove near where Cecilia lay gasping and wincing.

I walked forward, keeping my gun out. Just in case.

The woman had been stabbed. A bloody knife lay to the side. Streaks of crimson crisscrossed in splatters. As I neared her, the more gruesome it all looked.

She'd been stabbed in the stomach, sliced over her neck. Cut on her arms, perhaps a payment for trying to defend herself.

"Cecilia."

She whimpered, looking up and seeing me at last. Keeping her head raised seemed too difficult, and with the gash on her cheek, cut from her eye to her jaw, I knew the girl was bleeding out fast.

"I didn't mean it."

I went still. Frozen in place as I crouched to hear her as she cried, I ignored the sickening squelch of her tears mixing with her blood. Her tear ducts were torn with the position of the cuts. It was gross. Macabre. Hideous.

But I had a strong stomach.

"You didn't mean it?" I asked.

She sobbed, crying softly. Slumping to the ground, she nodded with her head on the bloody floor. "I didn't mean to have him killed."

"You helped kill Luka?" I asked.

Now she shook her head the best she could with her neck so wounded. "No. But he took my glass."

"What?" I felt dizzy with the adrenaline rush.

"Luka drank from *my* glass. I'd asked for it specifically to avoid alcohol. And he… he took it by accident and died."

I scrambled to understand. "What are you saying?"

"I'm sorry, Renzo. I'm sorry that Luka died. That your brother is gone. Just because he drank from my glass."

I clenched my teeth together, stunned speechless. "You're certain?"

"Yes. I didn't want any alcohol because of the baby. That's why I kept track of what drinks I had. And he took mine by accident."

Holy shit. A baby?

"Cecilia…" I shook my head, struggling to keep up.

"I won't make it, Renzo." She squeezed her eyes shut tightly. "I don't know why you're here, but I want to tell someone how sorry I am. For all of it."

"Whose baby?"

"Mine." She lowered her hand to cover her stomach and cried harder when her fingers slipped over the bloody wound. "Ours." Her stomach was flat. She wasn't showing the swell of carrying a baby, but I took her word for it. Deathbed confessions always seemed too starkly sincere and accurate.

"Yours and Luka's?" I asked.

"No. I had… I fell in love before I was arranged to marry him. And I had an affair."

I rubbed my hand over my face, bewildered and at a loss for which question to ask next. So many questions pinged in my mind, and I couldn't think fast enough. She was dying. She was eager to tell someone her truth, and I had to listen.

"I ran to hide."

"Did your father know?"

She sobbed. "I just wanted to hide and have my baby, but I was so scared. I didn't know who wanted me dead, but I should've realized…"

"Realized what?"

No words came. She struggled with labored breaths, and I grabbed her upper arm to shake her from passing out.

"Cecilia?" Giulia stepped closer. Her face was sober, full of concern and shock. She walked closer, perhaps planning to help.

The slender woman opened her eyes. With a vacant, trancelike stare, she seemed focused on Giulia. Yet not. The hazy, slurred tone of her drowsy speech suggested she was about to fade away completely.

"You."

She glowered at Giulia with such delusional hatred, it was as though she accused Giulia in all her woes.

"Cecilia…" Giulia stayed back, shaking her head with a sorrowful expression.

"I wish…" Cecilia gasped, closing her eyes tight before wrenching them open with an even crazier glare. "I wish this baby I carried would have lived." She opened and closed her mouth, struggling to breathe. "I wish my baby lived just to piss you off, you filthy bitch."

"Cecilia." I shook her arm too, trying to dislodge her frantic attention on Giulia to answer me. "Whose baby is it?"

She closed her eyes and kept them closed.

"Who killed Luka?" I shook her arm again.

Her chest ceased rising.

"Cecilia!" Again, I jerked on her arm. "Who stabbed you?"

"Renzo."

I whipped around to see Giulia. She still stood behind me, on the lookout. Glancing around the room, her small pistol in hand, she remained cautious.

She'd taken her weapon out of her pocket to have my back, and knowing that she was smart and quick enough to know this might still be a dangerous scene, I snapped back to attention.

I wouldn't be getting any other answers from this dead woman.

Cecilia Romano, and her bastard baby, lay dead on the floor. Bled out, lifeless, and never again able to shed any light or provide any clues on all this grisly drama that surrounded us.

"Fuck." I stood and stared down at the woman I might have had to marry. No guilt filled me. She hadn't been mine to protect. I hadn't failed her.

The only remorse that could hit me was that of not getting here sooner. To see who'd attacked her and wanted to end her life and that of her unborn baby's. To know who she'd had an affair with.

Anything. I felt thwarted, too late in learning anything that could help me.

If I hadn't stalled, maybe we would've gotten here quicker. If I hadn't stopped to kiss Giulia and proclaim my commitment to a future with her, if we hadn't attracted the attention of the Greeks on the road…

All of it.

"Renzo, we should go," she said.

I nodded, unable to look away from Cecilia and know that she couldn't help.

I was so close to knowing what happened. I could feel it. The truth was at the tips of my fingers, and I'd lost it.

"Yeah." I exhaled, looking over Cecilia's body for any other clues. We couldn't report this. Doing so would reveal that we were here, looking for answers. I should've felt bad to walk away, but that was all I could do. Giulia was right to be worried. I was grateful that she'd held on to common sense that we couldn't linger. The killer could be near, or spying on us this minute.

That jolted me into action.

I couldn't stand around here where Giulia could be in danger. We both had to get out of here, but more than that, I had to protect this woman I wanted to make mine.

"Come on." I took her hand as I retreated. We both kept our eyes peeled and our ears open as we hurried back out the way we'd come.

Sooner or later, someone would come and find this scene. Giulia and I had left no trace of being here. I doubted the surveillance cameras could have caught us walking in. The killer had likely disabled them with swift cuts through the wires.

We weren't the only ones to walk in here and leave just as quickly.

Another death had been added to the count.

On one hand, we were lucky not to run into them as they killed Cecilia. On the other hand, I hated that we were still in the dark.

"It's got to be the same person who killed Luka," Giulia said as we got into the car.

I sped away, nodding while we both checked our surroundings. "I agree." When she didn't speak up again, I glanced at her. "Why'd she say that at the end?"

She shook her head. "I… I have no clue."

"She wanted her bastard baby to live to piss *you* off?"

Shrugging, she paused in looking around to make eye contact with me for a brief, startled moment. "I don't know what that means. I never befriended her. I never knew her. And I certainly don't know anything about her baby."

Me neither. But I intended to find out. This child had to be tied to this mess.

"We will figure it out."

This time, she took the initiative to grab my hand and hold it. "We will."

We. I liked the sound of that. In the face of death, she stood with me. And at the risk of causing so much upheaval with the relationship we'd dared to forge, she didn't seem eager to step back and let me figure this out on my own, either.

21

GIULIA

Saying that I wanted to help Renzo was easier said than done. I didn't know *how* to help. I wasn't sure what to do next.

My mother expected me to come home, but I had no inclination to return after seeing Cecilia like that. While it was shocking, I wasn't dismayed and traumatized. It had been harder to find Father dead in his bed than stumbling upon Cecilia bleeding out on the floor.

She wasn't a stranger, but she wasn't anyone I was close to, either.

As cruel as it was to think it, that was just the way things worked in our world.

"What did she mean?" I wondered aloud. Instead of trying to guess what I should do next, I latched on to the stupefying shock of Cecilia lashing out at me like that.

"I don't know if she *did* mean anything," Renzo said. "She was a second away from death."

"You think she said that like a delusion? Hallucinating as her body shut down?"

He nodded, but his brow remained furrowed. "Maybe."

"Now what?"

His slight huff of a laugh charmed me.

"You're fucking amazing."

I raised my brows. "How so?"

"You just take it as it comes. Seeing a woman stabbed to death, and you're still so… practical."

"I prefer to think of myself as pragmatic." I gave up my hold on his hand to turn and watch him drive. Even in this action, he looked so dominant, so rugged and in charge. His arm flexed as he shifted the gearstick, and I wondered if I would find everything he did sexy.

Or, perhaps it's easier to let my mind go to the gutter and lust for him instead of facing the threat of mortality that always seems so near.

"We'll go somewhere safe while I look into this affair she had."

I blinked, stunned yet not. He was taking charge—as expected. He was bringing me somewhere with him—unexpectedly.

"You're not taking me home?"

He deadpanned at me. "So Isabella can lock you up until your wedding?"

"She would not…"

He raised his brows in a challenge.

I winced. She might attempt that. "But taking me somewhere else would only make her more eager to act out."

Sobering quickly, he frowned at me. "Would she use your sisters as leverage to get you to do what she says?"

My stomach twisted at that thought, but I shook my head. "Uncle

Dario is there. He'll watch over them. And Francis, my guard, he'll keep an eye on them."

Renzo nodded. "Then it'll be my pleasure to keep you close and let Isabella freak out about being out of control that much longer."

He reached a small yet stately residence within the hour. As we rode there, we discussed who Cecilia could have had an affair with. Who could have killed her. Why these things were happening when they did.

It was freeing to discuss things so openly and candidly with him. He saw me as an equal, not an inferior woman.

By the time we arrived at this Bernardi vacation home, the water glistening from the sunset on the horizon, I was exhausted. Mentally, I was fatigued from trying to figure it all out and thinking up the what-ifs. Emotionally, I was worn down from this burning wish to just embrace Renzo and have faith that we could be together.

My mother's ultimatum remained fresh in my thoughts too. She'd assumed I was running away with Renzo, and his bringing me to his vacation home was a signal that I was.

I couldn't. Not yet. We had to know who had done what, and then we could react.

Staying with him felt right.

He led me into the home, holding my hand, and I knew that the more he gripped me like that, the further I'd fall for him. It was a simple, almost casual touch, but I treasured the possessiveness behind it. Like he feared ever letting go.

"Dean," he said into his phone as we entered. "I need some information." As I yawned, he frowned at me. "Hold on. I'll call you back in a minute."

He hung up and studied me. "Are you tired?"

I shrugged. "I haven't been sleeping well."

He sighed and kissed my brow. "That makes two of us." Leading me to the master suite, he pulled back the covers on the huge bed and gestured for me to lie down.

I didn't. "Where are you going?"

He crawled onto the bed, showing me that he wasn't going anywhere.

I smiled, glad that he wanted to stay near me. After sliding off my sandals, I lay on the bed.

I wasn't too sleepy, but this sensation of feeling trapped and hopeless dragged me down. Closing my eyes was bliss. Hearing his voice as he talked to his man soothed me. Feeling the warmth of his body pressed next to mine was a rare treat that I wanted to cherish forever.

Renzo grounded me. Being with him like this, just decompressing and letting him arrange to obtain information about Cecilia's affair calmed me. This connection between us wasn't only sexual. He was an anchor that I never knew I could find.

But how can we stay? I saw no easy way forward to avoid marrying Nickolas where I could remain with Renzo. Running away was my first plan that made sense. But that would push me further from him.

I had nowhere to go with him.

I had no future to count on.

Just like Cecilia, I was a pawn. That was what our lifestyles dictated.

And it was to those sad, sobering facts that I dozed for a while.

I woke to find Renzo staring at me. He was no longer on the phone. Lying side by side with me, he gazed into my eyes with a calm yet deep intensity. As though he wished to see into me, to see my soul and hold me close. His hand drifted over my head as he continued to gently brush my hair back.

"How long have you been staring at me like that?"

"Not long enough."

I sighed, loving that he wanted me for longer. Forever. "Renzo, there's no way we can—"

He kissed me, silencing me with his mouth. "Stop. Stop giving up hope."

"But I am losing it." I never should've let myself think there was any hope between us.

"We will find a way to be together."

This time, I leaned in and kissed him, wishing he could be right.

"Because I want you," he confessed, his voice so gravelly and husky. "And for the first time in my life, I'm going for what I want." His kiss was rough. "What I need."

I crawled over to him, lying on top of him and kissing him harder. His words filled my heart. This pleading desperation to stay together goaded me to get closer. To unite with him. To surround myself with his affection.

"And I need you," he growled as he wrapped his arms around me tighter.

I clung to him. Keeping my hands over his shoulders and my left leg wrapped around his waist, I rode along with his quick roll.

He forced me onto my back, and I wasted not a second to reach for his shirt. I tugged it up, making him grunt when we broke our kiss. Without that layer of fabric hiding him, I reveled in the freedom to run my hands up his hard chest. Over his chest hair, along the ridges and dips of all his solid muscles. My touch spurred him to catch up, and as I pulled at the hem of my shirt, I lifted up to help him get it off.

"I need you more," I said between panted breaths as he reached for my bra. I shoved at my skirt, wanting to be bare for him. Wanting to be open and ready for him. It felt wrong to allow any layers to remain between us.

Already, my pussy was wet. I felt the dampness on my panties, and I couldn't wait to show him how much I'd yearned and ached for his touch there again.

Only him.

No man had ever felt me or entered me there.

And from the bottom of my heart, I wanted him to be my first *and* last.

My bra fell free, and the gritty growl that escaped his lips made me drip for him. Between the ache of my nipples and the tension banding so tight low in my stomach, I was so desperate that I became clumsy with my skirt. My fingers shook. My hands lost coordination.

I wasn't the only impatient one. With a rough grunt, he lowered me on the bed and swatted my hands away. Taking over, he yanked my skirt and panties down. I writhed, moving my hips and legs to get them all the way off, and instead of losing contact with him, I framed his face and clung to him so I could kiss him as he went even lower.

First, he covered my breast with his mouth. His lips sealed to my flesh, and with my nipple fully sucked in, I keened and arched my back.

"You need me?" he teased as he switched to my other breast and did the same.

"Yes. Please, Renzo. *Please*." I slid my fingers through his hair and held on tight to the soft, dark tresses. Keeping his head to my breasts ensured that the exquisite sensation of his lips and tongue wouldn't stop. And he didn't disappoint. Alternating between my breasts, he loved on me, pushing me close to an orgasm. But that wasn't all.

He fingered me, sliding his digits into my pussy and stroking me with a steady, firm drag that drove me wild.

"I need you, too," he said as he lifted his head from my nipples. They glistened from his saliva. Dusky pink and shiny with moisture, they stood as hard points. I wished he'd go right back to them, but he moved too fast.

He had something else in mind. Another first for me. As he lowered on the bed and hoisted my thighs over his shoulders, held as wide apart as he wanted them, I tried to prepare for the torture of his mouth on my pussy.

I cried out, fisting the sheets as he sealed his lips over my folds and swiped his tongue from my taint to my clit. He didn't miss a spot, sliding his hard, soft tongue over my sensitive flesh. A filthy moan left his lips, and I felt the rumbling vibration from his naughty kiss there.

"Oh, fuck, Renzo," I moaned, closing my eyes.

"Watch me." He paused only to order me that. His mouth returned to my cunt, and as I stared at him, he ate me out with a ravenous appetite. Slurping. Sucking. Even nipping. He tortured my pussy with long licks. Then he funneled his tongue inside and coated his face with my cream.

When he moved his focus to my clit, I cried out over and over, lost in the drowning pressure to explode for him.

"You need me like this, Giulia?" he asked with a wicked glint of mischief in his eyes.

"Yes. Oh, my God. Yes, Renzo." I panted and watched, turned on even more by maintaining eye contact.

He doubled down, making love to me with his mouth. Pushing his head up helped drive in the force of his touch, and I trembled with the need to come. "Please, Renzo."

I would never stop begging for this man. And he seemed to know it, too.

He dragged his hands down my thighs until he cupped my ass cheeks. His grip was unforgiving. His nails bit into my flesh, and as he squeezed, parting my ass, it drove me wild. Holding me closer, he growled and ate at me until my orgasm burst through me.

I screamed, clenching my eyes tight as the bliss speared from my pussy to the rest of my blood. Satisfaction was swift and sweet, and as I floated on the high of coming, he lowered my legs and hurried to remove the rest of his clothes.

"I needed a taste, Giulia," he rasped as he stood to the side of the bed.

I locked my gaze on his dick jutting straight out from the dark hair around the root of the shaft. Licking my lips, I fought through the fading waves of my orgasm and crawled toward him.

"Maybe I need one too," I taunted.

Before I could do more than pump my fingers up and down his veined hardness a couple of times, he chuckled darkly and caught me in his arms.

"Later." He spun me until I was on my knees on the bed again. He crawled up behind me and urged me up the mattress until we'd reached the headboard.

"Next time," he promised before kissing my neck and pushing his chest flush to my back.

I groaned, arching back to him and turning my face to kiss him. As we locked lips again, he rubbed his dick between my legs. I tasted myself on his tongue, and I moaned, then cried out. He notched his cockhead at my entrance. With his arm banded over my stomach, he paired his deep thrust in with a pull of my body back toward his.

He was seated. All the way in. The steady, hard push stole my breath, and I panted as I waited to adjust to the delicious stretch.

"Oh..." I growled it, feeling every inch of his hard length pushing in and filling me.

"I will always need you," he swore. As he pounded into me from behind, he reached lower to rub firm circles around my clit.

I was still coming down from my first orgasm and wasn't prepared for another so soon. Especially not a harder one.

"And I need you to come for me," he ordered as he sucked on my neck.

I leaned back, nodding the best that I could as I gripped his head and held on tightly. Arching into him, I tried to get there faster. I wanted to milk that big dick that he pushed into me faster and harder. I wanted to push him to lose himself in me and fill me with his hot cum.

"I need…" He growled, rubbing my clit firmly.

The first waves of bliss consumed me, and I fisted his hair as I let it sweep me away.

"Fuck. Yes." He drove in hard, once. Twice. And he came. I felt every twitch of his cock. I sensed his thighs trembling and shaking behind me. His breath came hard, whipping my hair aside, and with his strong arms around me, he hugged me close and pulled me to fall with him on the mattress.

Held tight in his arms, I caught my breath and waited for the rush of endorphins to settle within me.

And with him snuggled in, his warm, taut body stretched flush with mine, I realized we were on the same page.

I needed him.

And I feared I always would, no matter how many obstacles stood between us.

22

RENZO

Renzo

Giulia and I showered together, and even though I wanted her again, I knew she was exhausted. She hadn't napped for long, and after having sex again, twice within the hour, I took pity on her and let her rest.

It felt like a rare treasure to have her in my bed and know that she'd be there when I woke up and reached out for her.

The first time I'd taken her, I wasn't surprised that she'd run off. I'd fucked her so unexpectedly that night. Now, though, things had changed. Our tenuous relationship had evolved into something more, and I was confident that she'd linger.

Besides, she couldn't run away this time. Not easily. We'd driven up the coast for three hours to reach that Romano property where we'd found Cecilia on the brink of death.

I tortured myself by watching her sleep for a little longer. If I could be honest with myself, I'd admit that I was smitten. I would confess that I was utterly besotted with this woman.

My enemy. And at the same time, my other half.

As she rested, trusting me to be near her while she was at her most vulnerable state of unconsciousness, I thought back to what we'd learned earlier. I couldn't understand why Cecilia had verbally lashed out at Giulia when she approached.

Sometimes, death did funny things to people. I'd killed a few to know that in that moment before the ultimate end, strange things could be blurted without any censure, sometimes without any filter of making sense, either.

When I thought more on how Cecilia confessed to carrying someone's illegitimate child, I considered Giulia with that description too.

I'd fucked her three times now, three occasions of my flooding her with my cum. If she were to become pregnant with my child, it would be an illegitimate baby as well. Born out of wedlock. Conceived before she'd been married.

I wouldn't let her have my child with someone else. Over my dead body would another man raise my daughter or son. More than that, I hated to think of Giulia attempting to raise a baby on her own, without my help or resources, if she should try to run away from her engagement to Nickolas.

Knowing she could be knocked up still didn't prevent me from wanting her again. Being this close to her sleeping in one of my spare shirts, I was tempted to wake her up with my cock or mouth.

I would never stop wanting her.

And that wasn't fair to either of us. I intended to keep her—forever, and if we were to have a child together sooner than later, I would rather have done it properly, with the protection of her being a Bernardi.

I huffed a quiet laugh as I got out of bed without waking her. It was still early, just after dawn, and I wanted to entertain my thoughts apart from her and let her sleep in.

An Acardi becoming a Bernardi.

It sounded ludicrous because of what we'd been told all our lives. Both of us were trained to loathe each other, but now that we were together, it seemed so stupid, a waste of energy and anger.

I left her sleeping and retrieved my phone. My call to Dean ended four hours ago, before I woke Giulia from her nap. Since then, we'd fucked, showered, eaten, and fucked again. It might have been more like five hours when I considered it, and I had no doubts that Dean would have some information for me.

I'd instructed him to let me contact him, versus the other way around. I figured it would take him a while to have any answers for me.

I stood on the porch outside, looking over the railing to watch the moonlight reflect on the waves at sea.

Dean answered quickly, and he confirmed that he had news.

"It wasn't terribly difficult to get some intel," he explained, "because the tests were already requested."

I had no doubts about his ability to secure a hacker to find any electronic medical tests. This capo, this right-hand man, was invaluable and damned skilled at anything I asked of him.

"Requested by whom?" I asked.

"Marcus Romano."

I raised my brows. *Huh.* That at least proved that the old man knew his daughter was pregnant. "So he was aware that he was giving Luka a bride who wasn't virginal."

We weren't often so archaic to have brides prove their virginity. Some Families still had a doctor or other delegate to perform a manual check that the women were virgins. Others had the habitual showing of the bloody sheets. More often, it was implied. A hymen could break from other means, and I bet many cases of virginity were lost when the woman pleasured herself. It was only when infidelity was rumored, when women were caught in the act of having sex before marriage, that it became such a big deal.

Or, like in Cecilia's case, when she was confirmed to be carrying a baby before her wedding.

"Not only that," Dean added, "but Marcus Romano paid to have these medical results hidden."

"Damn." That made me more suspicious. The Romanos were already shady as hell, but this was not a mere omission of truth. It was a deliberate coverup.

"So, yes, Marcus wanted to hide the fact that Cecilia was pregnant when she married Luka. His motivation for that is yet to be uncovered."

I bet he won't tell why, either. However, this could've been a bargaining chip Giovanni could have used against Marcus. I wouldn't be marrying Cecelia. No one would. She was a corpse now. But if Giovanni knew about this baby, maybe he wouldn't have entertained even the possibility of my marrying her.

"The test results also confirm that the baby is a boy."

A son. *It was a boy.* I hadn't told Dean yet that I'd found Cecilia dying at the place. Word would spread soon enough, and even though I trusted Dean, I didn't need to complicate what the man focused on.

"And the father?" I asked.

He cleared his throat. "I don't have that information yet. The paternity testing has been ordered," he confirmed. "But it's not conclusive yet."

"Dammit."

"And I imagine that when that test is concluded, Marcus may want to erase evidence of it. I will keep my eyes open for it. The IT specialist I have tracking these documents and lab work orders will watch it closely, but in the meantime, no identity has been provided for the father."

Hmm... I agreed with him. If Marcus wanted the father's identity to remain a mystery, he had to have a damned good reason for it.

Maybe... I cringed at the first thought that entered my mind.

Maybe it's his. It seemed so ridiculous, so far-fetched and out there, but once the thought hit me, I couldn't ignore it.

Cecilia's child might have been the result of incest. If Marcus—or Nickolas—fucked her, that'd be incest as a father-daughter or sister-brother incident. That would surely be something to cover up and hide. If Marcus or Nickolas fucked their own blood, then of course they'd have a motivation to cover it all up.

Then why offer her in marriage to Luka?

"As soon as the paternity test results are in, I will forward it to you via a text, if you'd like," Dean offered.

"Yes. Please. I appreciate that. I feel that the identity of this man will be a critical development in figuring out who killed Luka."

"I agree," he said. "I think that this has to be a significant connection."

But to Rocco Acardi too? And Isabella?

I sighed, wishing I had more information. I couldn't explain why, but I felt like I was running out of time to figure this out.

Seeing Cecilia dying was a startling moment, but as hardened as I was to witnessing death, I wasn't upset. I wasn't stuck in a traumatic reaction to that woman dying, but it had served as a stark reminder of how short life could be.

How short the rest of my life could be, and I didn't want to lose a second of it that I could share with Giulia. It was useless to wonder how or why we'd connected so quickly and deeply. We had, and there was no going back from it.

But time was also running out, it seemed, for the killer. Assuming that it had to be one person, the same person, they were changing up their speed. Luka was killed at his wedding, then by the time his funeral passed, Rocco was dead.

Cecilia was only killed today, and viciously, in a different manner. No poison was used on her and her unborn baby. Slashing at a person and murdering them with a knife was a much more personal means of killing. Passionate.

And it worried me that the killer was getting out of control. Whoever was picking off these prominent people in this criminal world was getting desperate and changing up their methods.

If that suggested more danger to us, to me or Giulia, I had to remain on guard and be even more alert.

She won't be going home at all. Giulia didn't realize it yet, but as soon as she woke in the morning, I'd need to explain it all.

I couldn't, in good faith, take her back so she could live at the Acardi residence. I couldn't lose her. She might trust that guard, but I didn't. I especially couldn't trust Isabella if she was so set on arranging Giulia to be with Nickolas.

Who might have fucked his sister. It seemed like a big conclusion to jump to, but I couldn't ignore it now that it had entered my mind.

"This is all such a fucking mess," I mumbled to myself as I headed back inside. I'd hung up with Dean several minutes ago, and I debated calling him back to just talk this out with him. To hear his opinions about *all* of it.

Sooner or later, I'd need to rely on him to help me with Giulia. She would remain with me. I made up my mind there. And I had to have some assistance in keeping her away from Giovanni.

Until he explains this stupid rivalry.

It would have to end with me and Giulia. We would have to start a new generation. The past could stay back there. I had to focus on the future I wanted.

I walked back into the master suite, ready to get into bed and hold her for the rest of the morning.

But she wasn't there.

I narrowed my eyes, looking around the room and wondering how in the fuck she'd run off this far from home.

And why.

We were meant to stay together. She fought it more than I did, but I couldn't blame her for that. All her life, she was trained to know she can't change anything about what was expected of her. I had to do that. I had to step up and handle this demand for change and insist on our having a chance to stay together.

I ground my teeth, peeved that I would need to work harder to convince her.

When I stepped closer to the bed and spotted her earring, a small diamond stud, I grew worried. It wasn't a clear sign of her struggling. The bedsheets were already tangled from having sex, but I tried to look at the room for any hint of a fight.

Did she run?

Or was she taken?

All I knew for a fact was that she wasn't here.

And that was the only place where she belonged. With me.

23

GIULIA

Giulia

I woke to a firm grasp on my upper arm.

Again? So soon? I swore that I'd just closed my eyes, that we'd just had another hot, intense round of lovemaking. I wouldn't protest, though. I was already addicted.

I was a goner for my enemy.

As I came to, lazy to open my eyes, I rolled into Renzo's grip. He pulled on me, roughly, but that didn't alarm me. I was quickly realizing how needy and impatient of a lover he was. And I enjoyed every gruff bit of affection and desire he showed me.

"Shh."

What? Who said that? Warnings blared in my head, and as I opened my eyes, I saw a very real reason to be alarmed. Someone else had spoken. And it wasn't Renzo.

Three burly, tall men dressed in black had trespassed into the room.

As I opened my mouth to scream, to call for Renzo, one slapped his gloved hand over my mouth.

It was too thick of leather to bite through and cause this man enough pain to release me, but I tried. My screams were muffled. All the curses and shouts I flung at them faded to mumbled noises that wouldn't alert anyone.

A frantic glance to my left showed that I was alone on this huge, messy bed. But then I wasn't even in it myself any longer.

One man hauled me up by grabbing my arms. A third handled my legs. Together, they gagged me and tied me at the wrists in such an efficient manner that I knew they'd done this many times.

Mafia thugs. Soldiers who'd been trained to kidnap.

But who?

I fought the best I could, too damned determined to stop this fucking routine of being used and moved and controlled by men. Wriggling and bucking didn't slow this trio down. Not at all. They were too strong. Too practiced. And too eager to follow the orders of whichever Mafia lord had instructed them to snatch me right out of Renzo's bed.

How'd they know where to find me?

Who sent you to take me away?

Where is Renzo?

Is he okay?

Are they coming for me because we found Cecilia dying?

What is going on!

I couldn't rationalize an answer to any of my questions. They bombarded me as adrenaline kicked in. I breathed too fast through my nose, and my sinuses burned with the rapid inhalation on top of the musty stink of the rag they'd used to secure my silence. As my heart raced with fear and anger, I lost control of any calm, any steadiness that I could bank on right now.

I couldn't freak out. I had to stay in control of my emotions. Of my body. The more I repeated that mantra, I brought myself down from the roller coaster of panic and shock.

From sleeping in to taken away. It was mental whiplash, but I fought against the all-consuming terror that threatened to make me freeze up.

They rushed me out of the Bernardi vacation home and tossed me into the backseat of a car.

Driving was another guard, and I recognized him as one of the brutes Renzo's Family employed.

For fuck's sake. I glowered at the other three men. Two caged me in while I rode in the backseat, and the tallest one had taken the passenger seat up front. All four men worked for Renzo's Family. I'd been kidnapped by Bernardi soldiers. Taken as I slept at a Bernardi residence.

My anger shifted. A deep, seething rage slowly filled me.

As if I needed a fucking reminder that I'm the enemy. I didn't want to know how Giovanni knew that I was sleeping with his son. My mother had caught on to a partnership. She'd gotten word of me riding with Renzo when the Greeks tried to hold us up on the road. If she could hear about my being near the enemy, it seemed fit to assume that Giovanni would also become aware of the situation.

Having me kidnapped to keep me away from his son didn't sit well with me. Not at all. I heard how overbearing Gio was when Renzo let me listen in to the call in the car. That conversation told me enough about what kind of a dominant, control-freak sort of Mafia Don he was.

Maybe it was stupid of me to think that Gio could simply call Renzo and tell him to get me out of their villa.

Or maybe Gio knew better than to assume his rebellious and independent second-born would listen to him.

But taking me like this? I glared forward, letting my fury keep me warm inside.

This is bullshit. However, I could rest easier with the fact that Renzo had to be safe. Now that I identified who'd taken me, I could relax with the knowledge that Giovanni wouldn't hurt his own son. Punish him, yes. It seemed the first punishment was to steal me right out of the bed I'd shared with him.

And still, I remained furious. All through the long drive closer to the city we both called home, I fumed. It was absolute bullshit for them to pull me out of bed the way they had. I wasn't some criminal scum. They didn't have to force me into this car and transport me like this.

What stung even worse was how I'd fallen asleep to the fantasies that I could believe in Renzo. That somehow, we would have a chance to be together. That we could live as a couple in the future. In that fantasy world, I'd be Renzo's lover. His wife, even, Mrs. Giulia Bernardi as I lost the tinge of association with my mother by giving up the Acardi name.

I'd drifted to sleep with that dreamy vision. I'd get my sisters under his protection, and we'd be a happy family. And as Renzo's wife, I would own these Bernardi soldiers. They'd listen to me. I would have the right to instruct them to do whatever I wished.

Not be carted around like a shackled prisoner.

Not stuck and silenced.

The entire drive back to the city felt long, and every time I shifted to get more comfortable with my hands cinched together with a zip tie, the guards beside me shot me a dirty look.

I lifted my hand to show them the middle finger. When one smirked, amused, I hated that I'd given him the satisfaction of seeing how irate I was.

Cool it. Just keep it cool and wait to lash out on them all when we get there.

It wasn't a great plan, but I'd stick to it. As they transported me, I let my anger build up inside me so I could release it when the opportune moment came. It finally did. Parked at an entrance to what had to be the rear of the Bernardi mansion, the engine was killed and the men filed out.

Two of them handled my exit, but as soon as my feet hit the ground, I sagged. Letting my deadweight surprise them, I ducked lower to dart under their arms.

Unfortunately, another soldier was at the ready, and his tackling hold would definitely leave bruises littering my back and ass. Together, the soldiers got me upright and the new one carried me inside.

They went so quickly that I struggled to mark which way we went, but I realized where they wanted to leave me.

We headed lower within the house, not up. They took me down flights of stairs, not into furnished rooms.

In a dungeon-like basement, the asshole who lugged me over his shoulder stopped. Then he leaned forward and urged my body to slam to the hard cement floor.

I gasped with the gag over my mouth, and the quick intake of metallic-scented air worsened the rawness in my mouth and throat.

Pain ricocheted through my body, and as the dull throbbing radiated from the impact of falling onto my ass and side, I did my best to ignore the dried blood on the floor. The odors of piss and shit hung in the air as well, and I didn't bother to wonder where I was.

They'd brought me to a cell. Likely, a place with no easy exits. Somewhere they'd previously tortured and killed countless others.

I wasn't prepared for one man to step forward and slice off my gag. Another tossed a bottle of water at me, but I didn't rush to drink it.

"Is this poisoned?" I snarled.

"The fucking cap hasn't been broken, bitch." The man who growled that stalked out of the room, shaking his head and complaining about how ungrateful I was.

"This is what I get for fucking him?" I asked the others. "Tortured and killed just because I slept with him?"

"Shut up," one of them warned, glancing over his shoulder at the closed door.

What's he afraid of? They're just doing their job. They don't care. They were told to get me and bring me here, and that's that.

"Gio put a goddamn hit on me? Because some stupid old rivalry between our Families makes us the enemy?" I huffed, letting the water bottle drop off my lap and roll away.

"Shut. Up." The soldier repeated it with so much emphasis, I furrowed my brow. He raised his and opened his eyes wider with the command.

Is he trying to tell me something? I was so sick of men ordering me around and telling me what to do. I'd lapsed with Renzo enough to trust him, to want to believe in him. But I wouldn't lower my guard so much to assume this random Bernardi soldier was trying to give me a helpful tip.

"Well, I know better than to waste my breath and energy screaming for help." I couldn't stop this sarcasm from coming forth. It was likely a defense mechanism, a deterrence from realizing how dire my situation was.

"Don't—" The other soldier shut up as the door's knob was twisted.

Both men turned to watch others enter the cell, and as they filed in, I got scared. Now, I felt terrified. With these Romano soldiers coming into my space, I realized what was going on.

Giovanni Bernardi must have heard that Renzo was with me, the supposed enemy, when all I was trying to do was identify Luka and Father's killer. I was trying to help. I was risking the wrath of my mother to side with their Family and freely assist them in this mystery.

But Giovanni hadn't stepped in and interfered by removing me from Renzo's side.

He'd gone so far as to tell the Romanos to collect me.

Fuck!

These Romanos could only be here for one damn reason. Nickolas was coming for his intended. He was sending his men here to retrieve me, and there wasn't anything I could do about it.

Running from them would be impossible.

Attacking them would be pointless.

They outnumbered me. They had weapons.

I was well and truly fucked, bound and captured to be sent off to the sadistic man my mother wanted me to marry so she could delude herself further with the chance of having power and more money.

"Good." One of the Romano soldiers acknowledged my presence with a curt nod. He wasn't speaking to me as he took in the visual proof that I'd been brought here. They were collaborating on this whole thing. "We appreciate your finding her," he told the Bernardi guard who'd firmly suggested that I shut up.

"We'll move her soon," he told them, leading his group of soldiers out of the cell once more.

Both of the Bernardi soldiers left with them.

As the door clanged shut, they left me all alone.

Stuck with the company of my worst fears coming true, I clung to the stupid thought that I'd been robbed.

I wished that I could've had more time with Renzo. Kissing his bossy lips. Feeling his hard, strong body holding mine. And melting under the comfort of his hand gripping mine as we talked.

It wasn't enough. I wanted more with him. I wanted it all with him. A lifetime.

But that was all we could have.

As soon as those men returned, I'd be taken to my fiancé. I'd be held somewhere to ensure I stayed put and behaved until they deemed me fit for our wedding.

Fuck that.

I'd kill myself before becoming Nickolas's wife.

I belonged to Renzo, with my heart, body, and soul.

No other man would ever take his place for as long as I lived.

24

RENZO

Renzo

"Giulia?" I called out as I searched the house. This place was large, designed for hosting large parties and accommodating big groups of guests at once.

I didn't know why she'd wander or give herself a tour. I didn't care if she did. This woman was already sneaking into my heart, so it seemed backward to give a shit if she felt nosy and wanted to snoop around.

The further I went through the house, my suspicions grew. No alarms had been set off. I'd made sure to keep the security system on because no guards were around to offer backup. I wouldn't be so stupid with her safety.

Yet, it seemed like someone had gotten in. Not only that, but they'd done so *with* access to deactivating and resetting the alarm system.

"What the fuck?" I muttered to myself. Her earring remained in my pocket. As soon as I saw the bed empty and found her piece of jewelry, I got dressed and set out to find her. This little piece of shiny metal seemed to be all that was left of her. Like she'd vanished into thin air.

"Where the fuck are you?" I whispered to the empty and silent house.

If she hadn't tried to leave on her own, intimidated by the depth of my feelings for her, or vice versa, then someone had to have come here and grabbed her.

Precisely to avoid my interference.

And with caution to avoid tripping the advanced security system this place was rigged with.

As I considered the infuriating idea that someone could have been watching us, spying on us to know that I'd taken that call outside with Dean, I let my anger build up. The need to destroy something filled me, so when the sounds of the alarm panel being engaged reached my ears, I stormed over there with my gun in hand.

I wrenched the door open, cutting off the guard who was inputting the numbers. On the stoop stood Giovanni. He raised his brows at me, expectant as ever, and finished his call. Always on the phone. Always in action somewhere and somehow as the remote leader of us all.

He stepped in, and I narrowed my eyes at his stern, almost annoyed expression.

"Yes. That will work. I'll call you back shortly." He lowered the device as he stepped inside the foyer, glancing around the space. I didn't get the impression he was searching for something. More so, he seemed to stall in confronting me.

"What the hell are you doing here?" He *had* come here for a reason. The man was too busy to make a three-hour-long drive for the hell of it.

The timing of his arrival set me on edge. He'd arrived just after I discovered Giulia missing. While it helped that she wasn't here, I didn't want her gone from my side. Sooner or later, I'd need to begin taking the steps to make him aware that Giulia would be with me, but that wasn't today.

"I came to speak with you."

I shook my head. "How the fuck did you know where I was?" Once the words flew out of my mouth, I growled and held up my hand to stop him from replying. "Never mind." It wouldn't be hard to track me. All the vehicles could be traced. He hadn't been happy with my explanation that I was leaving the city, and I bet as soon as I'd given him a proverbial fuck-you of leaving town against his wishes, he'd tracked my route.

"You are not to mix with that woman."

I narrowed my eyes. "What woman?"

"Don't play stupid with me," he warned, lowering his voice and sounding more sinister. "You know who I'm fucking talking about."

I set my gun down and crossed my arms. "Enlighten me."

He stalked over, but I didn't flinch at his hurried approach. It would take a lot more to intimidate me than my father scowling and rushing toward me with anger.

"I don't have to enlighten you, you spoiled punk."

"I thought I was supposed to be second in command now," I retorted.

"Then act like it!"

I shook my head, biting my lip as I realized he had to have caused Giulia to be absent from here. *You'll pay for that, you motherfucker.*

"How am I not acting like it? I don't hover over the capos like Luka did. I'm not a control freak. And shit still gets done. Maybe the men and soldiers in the organization will appreciate the respect and have a higher morale."

"Fuck morale. They'll do what we say, and that's the end of it."

"What the hell is this? You drove all this way to bitch at me about my supervision methods?" With a fleeting, tempting thought, I borrowed a page from Giulia's book. The lure of running away and forfeiting my role in this Mafia Family had never appealed more than it did at this moment.

"You want to act like a second in command, you should be focused on finding your brother's killer. I told you to avenge him!"

"I am!" I roared it, not caring how much he'd perceive this as the ultimate sign of disrespect. "I fucking am."

"Oh, you are, huh?" He sneered, looking away as he walked back a bit, like needing to shake off his frustration. "You're looking for Luka's killer while you're shacking up here with Giulia Acardi. The stress of the job is already getting to you so much that you need to take a little vacation with the daughter of our enemies."

I ground my teeth, fighting back the urge to punch his smug face. "Fuck you. I'm not."

"You're not fucking that woman?" He grunted. "Not what I heard. Not what the witnesses said. The Greeks burned down half the fucking road chasing you when you were so pussy whipped and distracted that you didn't pay attention to whose territory you drove through. Imagine my goddamn surprise when reports came in that you were taking Giulia Acardi out of town with you."

"It's none of your business who I sleep with."

"Yes, it fucking is!" Hands fisted, he came close again as though he struggled with the same desire to punch hard. "It is my fucking business when you choose *her*. Of all the easy pussy on the earth, you have to fall for her bullshit?"

"You don't know what you're talking about."

He smirked. It was such a wicked, maniacal expression that he looked unhinged. "I don't?" Shaking his head, he looked away again and muttered under his breath. "I know more than you. I know, without a doubt, that you cannot mix with that woman. Giulia is off-limits."

"Fuck you."

"No. Fuck you, you dumbass. She's bad news."

I narrowed my eyes, getting angrier by the minute as he badmouthed the woman I wanted to make my wife. "You don't know her. You know nothing about Giulia."

"I know enough to assume." He pointed at me, his face taut and lined with fury. "I know her mother. And I know that Isabella Acardi is bad news."

"Giulia isn't like her."

He chuckled darkly. "She isn't like her? How stupid can you be to ever think that Giulia isn't just an extension of her?"

"Giulia is not Isabella's pawn. She hates her."

He snorted another angry laugh. "She actually led you to believe that? How goddamn stupid can you be? I expect you to act like my second in command, and you're not going to do that when you're so gullible to be conned by that bitch—"

I punched him. Hard. Right in the side of his face.

In my peripheral vision, the guards stepped forward, tense and ready to act. But Giovanni halted them. As he staggered back, sliding his jaw from side to side and glaring at me with murderous intent, he lifted his hand to ward the guards back.

"You have no fucking clue what you're talking about." He fumed, glowering at me with such venomous hatred shining in his eyes. "You have no idea."

"I don't," I agreed hotly. "So why don't you tell me?" I was sick of wondering and guessing why a perfect woman like Giulia had to be so forbidden. Why she had to live with the label of being my enemy due to an old issue that set this rivalry in place.

"You don't need to know everything. Not now. All you need to do is follow my orders. I told you to find your brother's killer and seek justice. I told you to prepare for marrying Cecilia."

I lost it. Chuckling turned into laughing, and I caught myself before it became hysterical. "Cecilia?"

He slitted his eyes, waiting out my laughter. He couldn't be so stupid and dull as not to realize that I was laughing *at* him. Of all the things he could have said…

I shook my head, getting a grip on my knee-jerk reaction.

Marry Cecilia?

That wasn't happening. It wouldn't have been an option for me to follow through with even if she hadn't been stabbed. My heart belonged to Giulia no matter what anyone said about it.

"You tracked me. You had to know exactly where I was," I said as my dark amusement faded.

"What of it?" he demanded.

"You have to know I went to the Romanos' villa."

He tipped his chin up. "I did. The men saw the route you took. I wanted to assume those rumors about your having Giulia with you were false and that you were stopping in to check on your bride, since you'd found her."

"She was never my bride," I spat. "I never asked for her."

"I asked on your behalf."

This is stupid. It was pointless to argue about it now.

"Oh, yeah? Well, she's dead."

He froze, staring at me.

"Cecilia is dead. I found her stabbed at that place."

"Dead?" He sobered quickly. His anger faded, seemingly replaced with something like concern.

Worry.

The news of Cecilia being dead alarmed him.

"You—" He glanced back at the guards, almost as if he were wishing for someone else to handle this situation for me. As though he didn't know what to do with this news.

"You cannot. Don't, Renzo. Stay away from that woman." He turned to leave. "Stay away from the Acardis. You'll never escape her wrath."

"Giulia's?" I followed after him, rushing after him as the guards hurried to the door to open it for him. Giulia had no wrath.

"Leave it alone," he warned.

"Gio!" I grabbed for his arm, but he wrenched out of my reach. "What are you talking about?"

He strode outside, heading for the car he'd been driven here in.

"Gio!" I yelled it, furious with his riddles. "Where is she?"

No doubt remained in my mind. He had to know where she was. With the use of the security system here and the tracking on the car, he was likely the one who'd arranged for her to be kidnapped, right from under my nose. Other than attacking him again and tackling him to the ground to pound out answers with my fists, I had no options. I was clueless, suspended in the dark, with too many questions he wouldn't answer.

The guards would outnumber me and side with their leader if I used violence against him. And that was a delay and obstacle I didn't need to deal with when finding Giulia was my goal.

By the time I reached the last step of the path, running toward the drive, the doors were slammed shut and the car sped off.

I stared after them, breathing hard. I was livid, seething and growling with this live monster of anger burning up inside me.

I didn't know what the fuck he was talking about, but he had to know something about where she was.

Instead of fuming and doing nothing, I hurried toward my car and got in to speed back home.

I wouldn't give up on Giulia. I would never.

If Giovanni wouldn't tell me anything useful about where she might be, I'd need to look elsewhere.

I'd ask Dario. Isabella couldn't be trusted. I didn't need to hear that from Gio. I knew that she was shady.

Giulia had spoken highly of her uncle. I wasn't sure I'd respect the man after knowing he'd sent his niece to spy at that club, but she seemed more open to listening to him than she was to hearing out anything her mother said.

I'd reach out to him. The spare Acardi brother. Once I grabbed my phone, I tasked Dean with tracking Giulia's uncle. He had to be more trustworthy than Isabella.

As soon as I could meet with the man, I'd warn him of everything I'd learned. He deserved to know that the man Isabella arranged Giulia with might have done something no one would stand by. Nickolas could have slept with his own sister. And the Acardis wouldn't want someone like that to be united to their Family. I'd tell Dario anything to get Giulia back.

"Fuck." I rubbed my hand over my face and focused on speeding as much as I could.

This situation was turning worse by the minute.

I could only pray that Giulia was safe and doing all that she could to survive on her path back to me.

25

GIULIA

Giulia

The longer I waited in the cell, the more my hopes faded.

I'd made up my mind. I would die before becoming Nickolas's woman.

But I had no clue how to make that happen.

Renzo would know that I was missing. Hours had passed, and he would've realized that the bed was empty within minutes of their taking me out of that Bernardi villa.

And if he knew I was missing, he'd be hell-bent on finding me.

But then what?

His Family was the one that kidnapped me. I had to assume this was Giovanni's doing. He called the shots. He wasn't retired yet, and per that call I overheard, he didn't seem to trust Renzo or agree with his style of taking over what Luka used to handle.

If Renzo learned that his Family's men had snatched me out of that house, what could he do about it?

It was way too soon for Renzo to have obtained the loyalty of any of the men yet.

There was no way he'd be able to overpower his father's men. While Gio was in charge, he'd order these guards to keep me here and hand me over to the Romanos.

To Nickolas.

No. I've got to get away.

I couldn't fathom being with that man. Not for one second. Now that I knew how good it was with Renzo, I didn't want anyone else to ever touch me.

So far, though, they were stalling.

They moved me from one cell to another, and while this one had a door to close and lock, they left it open. One small mercy was the absence of blood and excrement on the floor, but I couldn't—and wouldn't—get comfortable.

I had to stay on guard, even though the soldiers drank and snorted coke in the bigger hallway space outside my cell. With the door open, I could hear and see them as they passed by, and more than once, they taunted me to join in.

"You sure you don't want to loosen up?" a Romano soldier teased. "I heard Nicky likes it hard and rough." The others laughed along with him. "Might make it easier when he breaks ya in."

I kept my lips clamped shut. They'd get no response from me. I wouldn't give them the satisfaction.

As I waited for them to make a move or to transport me, I tried to cling to the strongest sense of calmness that I could. I had to be logical and alert, not emotional and scared. Terror coursed through me. I was absolutely afraid, but I couldn't show it or let it get to me.

"Eh, they're still meeting," one said eventually when they discussed whether they should start more lines of coke or they'd need to move me to the Romano residence yet. "They always got their meetings and shit. We'll get a text when to bring her to the car."

The *they* these men referenced had to be Nickolas or Marcus Romano and Giovanni Bernardi. It should have helped to know who I could hate and blame for taking me from Renzo. But it didn't comfort me much. It hardly mattered who'd conspired to keep me and my lover apart. The biggest detail I had to pay attention to was getting out of this situation and avoiding being in the Romanos' custody at all.

Renzo's face stayed in my mind, and when I thought back to the strength that man gave me, I felt more confident deep inside. Just thinking about him helped my wounded heart. When I replayed the sweet, sincere words he'd shared with me, my determination to get out of here rose higher.

"I will always need you."

I didn't doubt him. I believed Renzo when he swore that his affection and desire for me would remain permanent. We might have started with a fling, getting frisky at the wedding and then when he snuck into my house, but it had solidly and steadily developed into something far more lasting.

Something like love. Forever.

I didn't have a chance to think and dream about him. My fantasies of his rushing in here and rescuing me faded.

At the sound of the doors being opened further down the hall, I snapped to attention. While it wasn't a commotion, the men who were drinking and snorting coke moved around. It seemed like some were leaving or expected to move out.

Another person was coming? Or leaving? I couldn't follow all that they said, and with only partial comments given, I realized they were likely speaking on comms units in their ears.

"We'll go get the trespasser," one of Bernardi men said, gesturing for his fellow guards to go with him. He paused, glancing at the Romano soldiers. "I assume you'll make sure she stays put?"

"Oh, yeah. Yeah, we got it covered down here."

After the Bernardi soldiers left to deal with whatever incident had come up with a trespasser, I lost hope. It couldn't have been Renzo. They would've identified him as someone other than a "trespasser".

When the Romano guards came into my cell, I tensed.

Screw having hope and staying calm.

I strained to breathe steadily as panic clutched me.

It was in their eyes. The naughty, greedy glint that sparked there told me enough. Their quick and sure approach promised that they were determined to share my space in here. As the leader unbuckled his belt and unzipped his pants, I scrambled back on the floor.

My wrists were still tied, but my mouth wasn't gagged. I could kick with my untethered feet.

"What—" I stopped myself from asking. I *knew*. I wasn't stupid. They were ganging up on me in here. Now that the Bernardi guards were gone, these Romanos wanted a sample.

"She's gotta stay a virgin," a second one warned as he pulled his erection out from his pants.

"But that doesn't mean we can't fuck that tight ass," another said as he forced me onto my hands and knees.

My heart thundered against my ribcage as I resisted. They swarmed in here so fast, all three of them eager to violate me the best they could while leaving my pussy for their Boss.

One covered my mouth with his hand as they shoved my nightgown up. My panties were ripped off next, no matter how fiercely I kicked and squirmed to get free.

They blocked off the door with the way they'd hurried in here. Bound and smaller, I was defenseless against all three of them coming at me.

"I want to fuck her first," the tallest one said as he pushed one man aside.

I fell to the floor, unable to break my fall with my wrists bound. The aches in my knees didn't last long. All I could feel was the utter terror of what they'd do to me. Before I could get upright on my own, the leader fisted my hair and yanked me onto my bloody knees.

"Open up, bitch." He smacked his dick against my cheeks, and I smashed my lips tighter together. Tears leaked from my eyes. His grip on my hair was brutal, tearing at my scalp, but I would not sob. I would not open my mouth for him to violate me. The only cock I ever wanted in my mouth was Renzo's. And if this fucker tried to force himself on me, I'd bite him. Hard.

"What's going on in here?"

The sound of the Bernardi guard's voice was my savior. He'd come back to the cells, scowling at the Romano men who shoved their dicks back in their pants. The man who clutched my hair tucked himself away before he turned to face the Bernardi soldier, but he didn't release me.

"Bitch was talking back," he explained, tugging me up higher by his hold on my hair.

I cried out at the rise, and as I lifted both hands to dig my nails into his hand, another cry reached my ears. Not mine.

But another prisoner's.

They'd captured Uncle Dario. He must have been that trespasser the

Bernardis were alerted to retrieve. With a rough shove, they dropped him to the floor near me.

"Dario?" I whispered, stunned and saddened that he was here. That they'd treat a handicapped and weakened man so brutally.

"Leave her alone," the Bernardi guard ordered. He was older, taller, and while I didn't recognize his face or his voice, I got the impression that he was in charge down here.

Under his command, the men filed out. It was a lucky save, but I didn't have time to dwell on the blessing of being spared from rape.

"Uncle Dario?" I licked my dry lips and swallowed hard as I hurried over to him. My knees ached, stinging with pinpricks of pain at scrapes and also the throbbing radiation of a deeper wound. I scrambled over to him panting on the floor. As soon as I reached him, I rolled him over to his side and winced at the beating he'd received.

They'd hurt him, causing contusions to swell up and slight scrapes to line his face.

He rolled over, breathing hard. I felt the warmth of blood from his stomach before I could see where he'd been injured.

No!

"Uncle Dario. What happened?" I didn't need him to explain that he'd been shot. That was evident. As he shifted, grimacing, I saw the hole in his shirt, a gap that was now stained with blood.

"I was…"

I blinked back the tears that burned my eyes. He didn't deserve this. Whatever happened, he didn't deserve this treatment. I didn't deserve their kidnapping bullshit either, but now wasn't the time to whine about the injustice of it all.

"I was trying to find you. Isabella made plans, and I couldn't let her do it."

"For me to marry Nickolas?"

He struggled to breathe. I couldn't be sure if he heard me, if he understood. I'd just witnessed Cecilia dying, and I couldn't believe that I was here holding my uncle as he seemed to near death's door.

He opened his eyes, slitting his lids so he could squint at me as he labored through the pain. "You must go. Get your sisters and take them away. The Acardi name needs to die out once and for all with this vendetta. It'll never end."

"What vendetta? What is going on?" I brushed back his graying hair to clear his vision. "Uncle Dario," I pleaded, "what is going on? What are you talking about?"

"Take your sisters and start a new life. New names and a new home. I've tried to siphon money into a fund that your parents never knew about. I started alternative investments when I was just the spare, and now you need to find it and leave. Take the girls and go."

I nodded, desperate to let him know that I would obey his dying wishes. I'd already planned to leave this life. "But why? What is happening?" So many deaths. Too many questions.

I was sick of not knowing.

"Your mother…"

I clutched him closer as he sighed and his breath slowed with a wheezing sound. Blood left his lips, and I realized he must have been shot more than once. "Dario!"

He nodded weakly, roused. "Isabella."

"What about her?" I demanded. I knew she had to be involved, but how?

"She was Giovanni's first lover."

I blinked my eyes open wide, not counting on that.

"She knew he was arranged in a marriage, but she thought she could sleep with Giovanni and win him over. Marcus was already married. But she wanted the Bernardi name and wealth despite his being promised to another."

"And she slept with him?"

He nodded again, even weaker. He was fading fast.

"She wanted Giovanni for herself, but he stuck with his duty and married Arianna as he was expected to. No one could have anticipated that they'd fall in love, and that made Isabella so bitter that she vowed to seek revenge. I think... I've always suspected that she killed Arianna all those years ago. As payback for Gio not choosing her over his arranged bride."

Holy shit! This was a hell of a bombshell to take, but as I let his words sink in, I knew this had to be the foundation for that damned rivalry that set me apart from Renzo.

"Gio loved her. Arianna. But I think Isabella killed her after Renzo was born. She couldn't stand it while she was married to Rocco, her second choice, and suffered from infertility until you were born years later."

It would take a while for this shock to filter through me. I didn't have time to sit here and ask for a history story. "But what does this mean now?"

"It means you need to go. Leave, Giulia. Save yourself and your sisters." His finger shook, and it was with that tremble that I felt the need to look down.

He pressed a small knife into my hand, and as I took it, I understood what he was doing.

"I suspected you were held here. Isabella mentioned meeting with the Romanos, and I wondered why she was heading here, so near the

Bernardi estate." He coughed, spitting up more blood as his breaths slowed. "I took a chance that getting captured would bring me to you."

I sniffled, letting my tears drip down on his bloody shirt. "Oh, Uncle." As I tried to hug him, so grateful and overwhelmed by his ultimate sacrifice, I held back from crying.

"Please. Go. Francis will help you get away. I beg of you, Giulia. Start a new family. A new life. It's long overdue." With those final, whispered pleas, he closed his eyes. Once, then twice more, he exhaled.

He was gone.

Dead.

I stared down at the only relative who'd ever tried to stand up for me. The spare brother, considered less than compared to my father when he was the patriarch. But also, the only man who'd ever attempted to raise me with courage while under the watchful eyes of my parents.

Go.

He'd begged it of me with his last breath, and I couldn't sink into a pit of despair now. I would mourn him. I would grieve for this giving man, but I had to heed his last orders first.

I stuck the handle of the knife between my teeth and sawed at the zip ties that bound my wrists. It took longer than I wanted it to, and with the tears that blurred my eyes as I looked over my uncle's corpse, I strained to work harder and faster.

I *had* to get away. I couldn't let his sacrifice be all for nothing.

As soon as the ties snapped, broken from my hasty cutting, I dropped my arms and shook out the aches. My limbs were numb, but as blood rushed through and my muscles could move free of the binding, I grabbed the knife once more.

Fisting it in my hand, I prepared to leave.

They'd have to come back soon.

And that would be my moment.

I'm sorry, Uncle Dario.

I stared at his lifeless body, overwhelmed with sadness and remorse that I'd lost him like this and would have to leave him here. I couldn't drag him with me to give him a proper burial and send-off. I couldn't spend another moment praying over him and telling him my sorrows.

I waited. Tense and bracing for a fight, I plastered myself to the wall next to the doorway.

The moment someone touched the doorknob, I locked my muscles and held my breath.

The panel pushed open, and I leaped forward, the knife coming out before me.

It was only one. A single Romano guard. Seeing that it was the man who'd slapped my face with his dick, I crouched lower and yanked my hand back, only to plunge the knife in again—upward near his groin.

Because I'd caught him by surprise, his reaction was stalled. I wasn't too naïve to assume it could be this easy. Already, he reached for his gun. With my lucky stab up near his dick, likely severing something down there, I'd rendered him almost speechless. But for good measure, I stood and gripped his head to bash his face on an upward swing of my knee.

Then I ran. With Dario's bloody knife, I sprinted up the stairs and refused to stop until I'd reached safety.

Nowhere seemed safe anymore. I only ever felt secure in Renzo's arms. I ran from his family home, though, knowing I would need to carve my own safe haven somewhere else in the world, far from the drama and danger that saturated our lives here.

26

RENZO

Renzo

By the time I reached the city limits, I felt like a tense bomb waiting to explode. Frustration welled within me. Speeding as fast as I could, I tried to stay in control and not let this urgency overwhelm me.

I was impatient to get home and figure out where Giovanni could have had Giulia taken and held. I didn't waste my time calling him. Demanding for him to tell me anything would be a waste of time.

He'd made up his mind. He was determined to stick to his old grudges with Isabella and the Acardi name regardless of how faultless Giulia was in whatever had pissed him off in the past.

It wasn't her fault she was an Acardi. Nor was it mine that I happened to be born as a Bernardi. Whatever made him so judgmental and biased had nothing to do with anything Giulia or I did in the present.

Dean called me as I neared the main Bernardi estate where Gio lived, where Luka used to live, and I answered, hoping he would have information for me.

"What is it?" I asked after I greeted him curtly. I didn't need to worry about hurting his feelings by being gruff. He was just as taciturn.

"You need to come to the house," he said. A shuffling sound on his end confused me. Almost like he was covering up his phone and hurrying somewhere.

Is he trying to hide? Trying to sneak around?

"I have information, but it's better if you come here and see... what I found."

I agreed and hung up as I sped up even faster. If any cop dared to pull me over, he'd regret it. Nothing could keep me from getting information that would lead me back to Giulia. Nothing.

I braked so hard that rubber peeled and screeched on the drive. Parking haphazardly, I grabbed my phone and ran inside. No guards stopped me. No one called out to me.

I sprinted inside, seeking out Dean. He'd instructed me to come here, but he hadn't told me where to go.

Calling out for him didn't seem wise. Since I'd punched Gio, I felt like I'd made myself something of an enemy. I was his son. I was still the second in command, taking over after Luka, but hitting Giovanni was a grievance I would have to answer for. I wouldn't be surprised if he ordered guards to watch me, to protect himself.

Of course, we'd argue and come to blows, but with my choice to side with wanting Giulia instead of simply nodding and going along with his orders to give up on her, I'd drawn an irrefutable line in the sand between us.

"Renzo."

I spun, finding Dean jogging toward me through the huge foyer space.

He wasn't out of breath, but he moved with an implied need to hurry. "This way," he said with a nod toward another hallway.

I trusted this man, and I didn't protest when he guided me through the house. Asking him what was going on wouldn't make a difference now. Without a word, I hustled with him toward the back of the mansion.

He took me down the stairs, and I dreaded the reason he might want me near the cells where we normally locked up traitors and prisoners. It was preferred to move and keep our enemies and foes further from our main and largest home, but the old underground layers that resembled an archaic dungeon had been built many generations ago for a good reason.

"I came back here earlier and saw several soldiers rushing out," he said, speaking softly and quietly as we slowed in the area of specific cells.

"When I came inside to see why the men might have been running out the entrance that's only accessible through here, I found this." He pointed at the floor inside one cell, and I sucked in a breath at the sight of darkness on the cement.

Blood.

Someone had been severely wounded in here. My first thought was Giulia. If she was the one who'd been injured and bleeding out in here...

"Over there." Dean wasn't imploring me to look at the large puddles of still-drying blood, but at a small item near the back wall.

I approached it, narrowing my eyes and wondering what he was concerned about.

As I crouched lower, my breath got stuck in my lungs again.

Slowly, I reached out and picked up the tiny diamond stud.

Giulia's earring. The other half of the pair resided in my pocket. It had come out in the bed at the vacation villa she'd been taken from.

She was here.

I looked back again, chilled by the idea that she could've been the person to lose all that blood over there.

"She…"

"I have not seen any sign of her anywhere on the premises," Dean said as I picked up the earring and paired it with the other one from my pocket.

"As soon as I arrived, I searched for her through all the cells." He cleared his throat, gesturing for me to follow him out of the empty room.

His report of not finding Giulia anywhere else here should've comforted me, but until I saw her and knew she was alive and well, I wouldn't lose this grip of fear.

We moved so hastily through the holding cells and the corridor that connected them. In our hurry, I knocked against a rudimentary table. Cigars were still smoldering. Numerous bottles of booze still held alcohol. And with a double-take, I spotted the remnant of a line of white powder.

Guards had been in here recently. If Giulia had been brought here, she'd been moved quickly.

"What else?" I asked him, following him out toward another storage area that was likely once a cellar for wine before a newer one was built.

"Him." Dean pointed at the floor, showing me a thick streak of blood that had dripped out of a cupboard area. "I noticed this when I ran through, and upon further inspection…" He pushed the small door open and revealed a body.

It wasn't Giulia. Knowing she hadn't been killed and shoved into this closet space was a relief. But she would be upset to see that her uncle had been treated with such disrespect.

Dario lay slumped in the small space, slanted against the wall like he was a sack of bones to dispose of later.

"Fuck." I raked my hand through my hair, stunned and horrified at the escalation of deaths here.

I'd *just* seen Cecilia dying. It hadn't been a full day since I'd spotted that woman bleeding out.

Dario seemed to have received a different, more immediate ending. Tucked away here on my family's property, he had to have been killed by a Bernardi soldier. There was no other explanation for why he'd be dead and stashed away here.

But... I couldn't connect the dots and assume that this meant whoever killed Dario was the same as whoever had ended the lives of all the others. Cecilia had been stabbed, not shot like it looked like Dario had been. And not poisoned either, like Rocco and Luka.

"Giulia..." I couldn't think past the utter confusion and worry eating away at me. Dread built within me, and I breathed through the panic taking over.

"She's not here, from what I can see," Dean said, seeming to realize that I needed the direct reassurance. "I think she was here, if that earring is hers. But she must have escaped."

"Have you—" I swallowed hard. "Have you heard from the others? The other guards and men?"

He shook his head.

"You haven't heard of any orders from Giovanni?"

Dean often worked alone, almost like an independent and free agent as my right-hand man. He wasn't tied to the stricter duties of patrol men and capos because he was expected to follow all my orders directly.

"No. I haven't heard from your father directly. I haven't been able to get any answers from the crew he orders the most, nor anyone in his personal security detail." He tipped his head to lead me upstairs as he retrieved his phone.

Finding Dario like this wasn't the end of it. He'd need to be removed. Buried. Dealt with. But none of that mattered as much as finding Giulia did.

"I came here right after getting word about those reports." He furrowed his brow, checking his phone then frowning as we climbed the stairs back up to the main level of the mansion. "If I can get reception…"

I stayed at his side, looking over at his phone as he refreshed the tabs. "You received information?"

He nodded, bringing me toward the windows at the back of the lounge area. No one interrupted us. Guests hadn't been staying here lately, and with whatever commotion had made the guards rush out that exit near the dungeon access, it seemed that all the forces were held up elsewhere.

I waited tense, agonizing seconds for Dean's phone to refresh, and once it did, I realized that he was uploading a copy of a document. A medical document.

"The hacker was able to get a copy of the paternity tests sent in for Cecilia Romano. They were ordered and paid for by Marcus Romano," Dean said, almost like needing to reiterate the facts that he already knew. As if I needed a summary.

"Paternity tests?"

I whirled back, facing Giovanni as he approached. For once, he was alone. No Bernardi guards came with him into the home. But he didn't come close with any clear indication that he wanted to shout at me again.

Shock and confusion showed on his face. Lines tugged on his features, and with a gaping open mouth and wide eyes, he seemed absolutely stunned.

"For Cecilia Romano?" he asked, as though speech was difficult. "You doubt she was Marcus's daughter?"

I shook my head. "Paternity tests for her child."

He furrowed his brow. "She was pregnant with Luka's child?"

Dean exhaled, still swiping on the screen to get it to upload. Since being down below in the cells, it had gotten locked with no reception. "No," he answered.

It was on the tip of my tongue to demand to know where Giulia was. I couldn't hold it in, no matter how caught off guard he was about hearing of Cecilia being pregnant.

"Where is Giulia?" I demanded. I wouldn't waste time asking whether he knew. He had to.

"She ran."

Fuck! While I was glad she'd run from whatever fate waited for her in the cell, that she'd run to safety, I feared this meant I would never see her again. Now, more than ever, she would make good on her desire to run away for good, like she'd hinted at when she was informed of the possibility that she might be Nickolas's wife one day.

"Why—"

Giovanni held his hand up, frowning deeper. "Cecilia was pregnant? When she was married to Luka? Before then?"

Dean nodded, holding up his phone higher. "Yes."

I turned, skimming the lines quickly. The results were in. And on the line identifying the father of her baby was a name I hadn't counted on seeing.

"Whose is it?" Giovanni asked, crowding in close to see. He sounded too stunned, stuck in disbelief, to catch up.

"Rocco Acardi," I read of the test on Dean's phone.

"Acardi!" Giovanni bellowed. He fisted his hands and glared at me.

Giulia's father. He was the one Cecilia had fallen in love with while engaged to my brother. He was the one who'd knocked her up before she married Luka.

I thought back to the impassioned, furious words Cecilia spat at her deathbed. When she lashed and snarled at Giulia that *she* would be pissed if the unborn son she'd carried from her affair with Rocco would have lived.

Because it would be a son? To take over the Family instead of anything Giulia would achieve through marriage?

It made no sense. I wouldn't have much time to think about it, though.

Giovanni swore and stepped up to me.

"Go." He licked his lips and shook his head, seeming more frightened and alarmed. "Go, Renzo. You must kill her."

I reared back, studying him. "Kill who?"

"Isabella." He nodded and grabbed my hand. "You must."

He no longer was shouting at me, no longer acting like he was upset with me. Now, he stared at me like I was his last hope.

"She's unhinged. She's crazy." He shook his head, muttering more curses that I couldn't keep up with. "She's... She's got to be stopped before she kills someone else!"

"What?" I asked as Dean looked between us, seeming as lost as I felt.

"She's..." He groaned and ran his hand through his hair. "Isabella Acardi. She must be stopped. She's gone too far. First, my wife. Then my son?"

I narrowed my eyes. My heart raced faster and faster the more he ranted these strings of nonsense. Or was it nonsense? If he was speaking the truth and he truly believed Giulia's mother had killed Luka…

"Explain," I ordered. "What the fuck are you talking about?"

He gripped my forearm again, as if a physical touch would emphasize it. "She is crazy. The last time a man chose another woman over her, she killed her."

"Who?" Although I had a sinking feeling who he was talking about.

Him. And my mother.

"I didn't stay with her. We were fooling around before I was arranged to marry your mother. And she didn't like it. Isabella was furious that I stuck with marrying your mother, and she became deranged when I loved her. She killed her, Renzo."

Rage swept through me. "Isabella Acardi killed my mother?" Arianna Bernardi didn't live long. I'd only had her in my life for four years, and I only had photos and videos to know her by with the few memories I'd formed before she died—supposedly, in a car accident.

"I never had proof," Gio admitted, shaking his head and lowering his gaze. "I could never prove it, not completely, but over the years, she gave me hints."

"She taunted you," Dean said, his glare full of fury. "For years, the security team dealt with her teasing messages and suggestions that she'd seen to Arianna's death."

Gio nodded, frowning.

"And you let her *live*?" I demanded.

"I felt that the best payback was to let her live with the fact that I still would not choose her with Arianna out of the way. That I'd rather be content forever with the memory of my wife, my love, than ever bothering with Isabella at all."

"You truly believe that Giulia's mother killed my mother?"

Gio sighed. "I do."

Dean nodded, added his input silently.

"And you suspect she's also killed Luka?" I asked, unable to believe this twist. "Why?"

"Because she wants to attack me. Us. Our name. In any way she can." Again, he gripped my arm, now holding both.

I wasn't sure if he held on to anchor himself or if he needed to emphasize his wishes stronger.

"You must end her, Renzo. You must."

I must. Because if Giulia ran out of here and had any plan to run home, where her calculating, murderous mother might be waiting for her, I couldn't risk losing her to the psychopath too.

"Go!" Gio ordered, releasing me with a shove.

Dean nodded at me, running with me as I rushed out of the house to hurry to the Acardi residence.

If she was safe somewhere else, I'd do what I'd set out to do so long ago. Since Luka's wedding reception.

I'd avenge my brother's death, and afterward, I would run away with my woman.

I didn't want to be tasked with cleaning up the messy remainders of my father screwing up with that woman.

I wanted to count on my future with the daughter of my enemy.

Because I wasn't sure if there was anywhere on this earth that could get us far enough away from this twisted, sordid drama spanning multiple generations. And neither Giulia nor I needed that kind of an obstacle to our love.

27

GIULIA

Giulia

I ran until I reached the road, amazed that I was able to flee on my bare feet for that long. The further I sprinted from the Bernardi mansion, the more determined I was to get away for good.

I'd go home and set up safer locations for my sisters. Marianna would help. Beatrice and Lucia enjoyed visiting a distant cousin, and I was sure that I could ask them to help keep them away from my mother, away from this place.

I didn't need all this wealth and pomp and fuss that came with being the daughter of an elite Mafia Family. My younger sisters didn't care for this lifestyle, either.

Regardless, I couldn't trust my mother with my life and future. I couldn't trust her with my sisters', either.

But I knew I wasn't alone. I'd trusted Uncle Dario, and he was now gone. Francis would be an ally. And Renzo would always have my heart and faith.

I'll run, and when it's safe, I'll ask him to come to me. To start over a new life outside the Mafia, if he can choose to do that.

Now that he was Giovanni's second in line, I wasn't sure if he'd be able to give it up. It sounded like he wasn't enjoying the change from being the spare to the next leader, the prince, but I understood that duty was defined differently for the men in our world.

First, get to safety. Then, plan for the future.

I flagged down a ride once I reached a busier road, and I was grateful for memorizing the number of my account to pay for the transportation.

The driver seemed suspicious of my bloody clothes, and even though I tucked Uncle Dario's knife under the nightgown, I felt his stare on it. Over and over, he glanced in the rearview mirror like I'd attack him.

"Do you want to go to... uh, the hospital or something, Miss?"

I shook my head.

When we neared the home, he swallowed and grew more nervous. "Um. I— Can I just, like, stop out here?" He eyed the gates and grimaced, knowing that this was a Mafia residence.

"That's fine. Thanks." I didn't wait for him to blather on nervously, and I exited the car.

The guard at the gatehouse raised his brows, and he hastened to unlock the entrance. I waved at him, which likely seemed even weirder, but I let him know that I was at least capable of acknowledging him. As if that would make me look less suspicious.

I'd been gone for almost two days. Returning like this didn't look good. I didn't care. With a deep determination to avoid my mother and get my sisters out of here, I held my head high and hurried inside.

"Giulia."

I slowed slightly as one of the butlers approached. He offered me a folded note, and he had the common sense to really keep his expression neutral. Not a single reaction showed on his face, and when he didn't bat an eyelid at my disheveled appearance, I exhaled in relief.

Taking the paper, I raised my brows at him. I'd dealt with the staff since Father died, and it was a hard habit to break. "Is my mother in?"

He shook his head. "No. She left for a meeting earlier and hasn't returned yet."

Meetings. I bet she'd gone to speak with the Romanos about my wedding to Nickolas. A ceremony that wouldn't happen.

"Thank you. Please arrange for a driver for my sisters."

He nodded and backed away.

I unfolded the paper as I hurried upstairs to find my sisters and order them to pack quickly. With what Uncle Dario said, it was clear that we couldn't stay here. Not without any trust to be held.

Giulia,

I will await your call for security. As soon as you relocate your sisters, contact me and I will come.

Francis

I sighed, calmer with this reassurance. Uncle Dario really had done all that he could. He'd thought ahead and seen to all these plans for us, and I fought back a swift wave of tears that burned my eyes.

I would miss him. Even though he'd tried to remain aloof, he'd always been there in the background, helping out and remaining independent of my mother's influence.

I didn't have my cell phone anymore. It was with Renzo at that vacation villa, unless he'd been taken farther from me. I knew he'd be looking for me, but I wasn't sure what Giovanni might have told him to keep him away from me.

I couldn't worry about that. With a backup burner phone that I kept in my closet, a just in case device, I added Renzo to the contact list. I would reach out to him. I wanted to plan a reunion, but first things first.

After texting the distant cousins about housing my sisters, I went to Marianna's room to order her to pack.

She already was. Beatrice and Lucia helped her stow things in her suitcases.

"You know?" I asked.

They ran to me, hugging me and worsening the tenderness of the aches where I'd been dropped to the floor.

"Before Uncle Dario headed out earlier, he said you would escort us to a, uh..." Marianna cringed.

"A 'vacation.'" Beatrice used air quotes, but as she stepped back out of our group hug, she noticed the redness around my wrists. She gasped. "What happened?"

I shook my head. I hadn't had time to think about what I'd tell her. Now wasn't the moment to explain, either.

"Are we going on a vacation?" Marianna asked. "Or...?"

"Just pack up and be ready to go."

"Does this have something to do with Father's death?" Lucia asked.

"Or how... weird Mother's been acting?" Beatrice asked.

I sighed, wishing I could drop to the floor and just avoid the stress of all these questions. Marianna was perceptive to notice how exhausted and worn down I looked.

"Both, I imagine." She ushered the younger two back into the room. "Regardless, we will listen to Giulia and follow her lead. She'll always know what to do."

Really? Do I? Will I? Her stout confidence in me fueled me to stand up straighter. After a firm nod, I drew in a deep breath and shoved away my moment of weakness. I was stronger than this. Sooner or later, I *would* succumb to the mental roller coaster. Seeing Cecilia dying. Making love with Renzo. Being kidnapped. Uncle Dario dying. The relief of running away. All of it. I was bottling it up, functioning because I had to, and I couldn't let up on that tight rein yet.

Only once we were somewhere safe, far from here, could I let myself *feel* again.

Back in my room, I stashed more clothes into my largest suitcase. We had to leave before Mother came back to the house, and without knowing where she was having her meeting or how long she would be out of our way, I had to hurry. And hurry. Faster and faster. Clothing fell and got tangled in the zipper of my case. Stuffing my most practical shoes into another bag was a clumsier attempt at packing. My rush knocked my purse to the floor, and I winced. It hardly mattered whether we took lots of items. Just enough to get by for a while until we could be settled somewhere else.

Now that I was acting on the plan to leave, to run away, it felt so surreal. Like this was someone else stuffing my things into cases in a rush. The moment to act on my future, to choose my path myself... I struggled to believe that it was finally here. That I was now poised to strike out for a different life.

I wanted one with Renzo, but there was no way to make that happen.

"And where do you think you're going?" Mother asked as she slipped into my room.

I sucked in a breath and held it. She'd surprised me. I'd counted on her being gone for longer, and that was my first mistake. Still, I wasn't here dawdling. I wasn't idling around. Without glancing at her, I continued to stash my things in my suitcase.

"I'd like to travel with my sisters. Before I'm a married woman."

She huffed, leisurely entering my room. Her pace was slow but measured, and feeling her stare on me made me nervous. She sounded too cool. Too calm and collected, like she had ultimate confidence that she held all the power in here.

"Oh. I see. You get out of town with that man and think you can just take off wherever, hmm?"

I clenched my teeth, refusing to make eye contact. If I looked at her, she'd see the barely veiled anger I kept within me at the sound of her voice. Antagonizing her wasn't what I wanted to do. Uncle Dario didn't have any proof to offer me when he claimed that my mother had killed Renzo's mother. But I didn't need it. I'd grown up knowing how strategic and cruel she could be.

"I am not a married woman yet," I reminded her, "and I would like to enjoy spending time with my sisters while I can." This seemed like the easiest deflection. The safest way to shut her down.

"You are not going anywhere." She slammed the suitcase shut and shoved my shoulder until I staggered back. I'd set Uncle Dario's knife on the vanity in the bathroom when I changed.

Dammit. I was defenseless, and the crazy look in her eyes scared me.

"You are *not* going to run off like this." She bared her teeth as she lifted her finger at me. The digit shook, trembling with the force of her anger.

"You will *not* run off, impregnated by Renzo Bernardi."

My jaw dropped open.

"I know you've been fucking him, running off like that with your lover."

"But I'm not preg—"

"Shut up!" she screamed as she lifted a gun out of her pocket and aimed it at my face. "Shut up, you little whore!"

"I..." I shook my head. I couldn't prove I wasn't pregnant in the same sense that she could guess that I was. We hadn't used protection, but still, this was an insane accusation to leap to.

"I'll be damned if my daughter gets a Bernardi when I never could."

Because you wanted Giovanni. You killed his wife because he chose his arranged bride over you.

"You're not going to fucking leave and foil my plans. You will stay here." She jabbed the gun at me. "You will abort any Bernardi baby you have." Another thrust of her gun. "And you will marry Nickolas Romano so I can get closer to his father."

Jesus. She was twisted. Hearing her plans for me pushed me over the edge. "Oh. You've got it all figured out, huh?"

"I do. I always fucking do."

I still couldn't antagonize her, but I couldn't dart to safety.

Stall her. Wait her out. I needed more time to react, to think, and to resolve this predicament. My own mother wanted to shoot me, but I supposed in light of all the violence and death she'd caused before, this was nothing.

"You'd really shoot me." I said it as a statement rather than as a question.

Her upper lip curled. "That's up to you. If you make a move to leave, I will."

"Because what's one more death, right?" I bit the inside of my cheek, wondering if I could get her to let me walk back to the balcony. The doors were open. If I leaned over the railing, could I get away like that, with the risk of broken bones?

She sneered. "One more death?"

"Yes. What's one more death on your hands? You killed Luka, didn't you?"

"It was supposed to be Cecilia! I intended for *her* to drink that sparkling water." Her neck strained as she clenched her teeth. Wild-eyed and furious, she glowered at me as I walked back toward the balcony.

"That fucking bitch was supposed to die, and do you know why?" She growled, breathing hard as she confessed. "Because she was carrying your father's son. His son!" The last part was a scream. Goosebumps broke out on my skin at her shout. That was how eerie she sounded.

"She was carrying his *son*," she fumed. "An heir, Giulia. That Romano bitch was carrying the son, the heir. The heir I could never give him."

It was her one job. With all the fertility issues, the miscarriages, and then, only having daughters. She'd failed epically in giving Father a son.

"All I could do was try to manage my daughters' marriages to the best of my advantage."

You wanted me to marry Nickolas so you could sneak into the Family too. To have Marcus's power since Father was dead now.

"But Cecilia thwarted it all. She screwed it all up. Once she gave birth to the bastard baby, the son your father put in her, she'd already be Luka's wife. That bastard baby would be passed as a Bernardi, and I will be fucking goddamned if Giovanni Bernardi ever got his hands on the Acardi wealth and power!"

I paced my steps backward, angling for the smooth surface of the balcony. Any second now, she could snap. She could be triggered to shoot, and at this close of a range, I'd be dead.

"I wanted to kill Cecilia." Mother explained like I was dull. "But Luka drank the poison by accident. I had it all planned. She was only drinking the sparkling water. I slipped it in from the waitstaff area, but that idiot Bernardi had to drink it instead." She shook her head as her eyelid twitched. "Then at his funeral, your father tried to leave.

He'd asked where Cecilia was. He wanted to go to her, to be with her now that I'd accidentally gotten her husband killed."

I narrowed my eyes, connecting the pieces of the puzzle.

"Did you...?"

She grinned evilly. "I killed Rocco. I had to when he was trying his hardest to fuck me over and start a new family elsewhere with his mistress. Then I drugged myself to throw off any suspicions."

"You killed Father." I tried to steady my breath through the adrenaline rush of fight or flight.

"I did."

"But you were drugged too."

She scoffed. "To make it believable. And if you dare to cross me, Giulia, if you even think about interfering with my plans, you'll join that short list of kills."

"That's all I ever was, huh? Just something to move around and dispose of for *your* benefit."

Nodding slowly, she brought her other hand up to the gun and held it firmly. "Yes. Until the very end."

28

RENZO

Renzo

I climbed up the trellis and vine supports to Giulia's balcony. It was becoming a habit, but I didn't care. This would be the last fucking time. The next time I wanted to see her, I'd walk right up to her. No need to be stealthy and sneak close.

She would never come here again. She wouldn't return to this house ever again. No matter where we decided to live, it would be together, in a home of our choosing.

Fuck Giovanni and Isabella. It was their mistakes and bad choices from long ago that tried to keep us apart. And it was because of their past that people were being killed now.

Giulia would not be the next victim.

As I reached the balcony and waited to pull myself up at the very edge, along the exterior wall of the house, I stayed tucked out of sight. A crevice in the drain system secured to the wall provided me a place to rest my foot, and I stalled there as Isabella continued to speak.

To shout and snarl. Every syllable of her ranting was laced with scorn, dripping with anger. I wasn't trespassing and breaking in on a safe, calm situation here, but I couldn't wait too long. If that woman was capable of killing my brother and her own husband, I had to get Giulia to safety *now*, out of Isabella's reach.

I'd heard plenty on my climb up here. Curtains flapped and flew back and forth in the breeze, but they served as a block. Vague shapes were visible through the gauzy material. Giulia and Isabella were forms, facing each other off, but they weren't engaged in any sort of combat.

The angle of one of their arms scared me. Like she was holding up a gun and aiming it at the other. Isabella's haughty tone and demanding words implied that she was the one threatening her daughter, and I had to be careful not to startle her and risk her pulling the trigger before I could shove Giulia to safety.

"I don't understand," Giulia said.

I commended her bravery, speaking loud and clear, but I caught the note of fear in her voice.

"You slept with Giovanni so long ago. It makes no sense to want to kill Cecilia now."

Isabella chuckled dryly. "Want to kill her? I did. After that fucking Bernardi fool drank her drink by accident, I *did* see it through and kill her." She grunted. "I wasn't going to. After everyone was all up in arms about Luka dying, I thought I'd let her suffer with her status. Marcus could deal with her. She could be a Romano and raise the heir of the Acardi name. But then he just couldn't fucking let it go. Your father worried about her. He wanted to know she was all right. Because he loved her. Not me. He loved her. He chose *her* over me."

"Maybe it was just an affair that would've petered out," Giulia argued gently.

As I readied to climb onto the balcony and lift myself over the ledge, I hesitated. Giulia backed up to the balcony. The nearer the women came, I saw how she was backing up. Her scent grew stronger the closer she got to me. Her hands were raised in a truce-like manner, and she kept her movements steady and slow.

She's stalling. Trying to get out to the balcony and escape. While I admired her scrappy determination to survive all the odds, I hated the idea of her jumping at the risk of injury or taking her own life. I doubted that was the case, but as she obviously exited toward the balcony I wanted to hide on, I had to bide my time.

"No. It fucking would not, you stupid whore. The second Cecilia screamed that Luka was dead, Rocco rushed up to her at her table to protect her, thinking she could be hurt. Then at Luka's funeral, Nickolas challenged Rocco with the accusation that he seemed too interested in his sister. All night long, he'd asked about Cecilia and tried to learn where she'd run off to. Rocco loved her, and I refused to let another woman interfere with my man again."

"Like Arianna did with Giovanni?" Giulia guessed.

"Yes!"

"But he was arranged to marry her. That's not the same as choosing her."

"No." Isabella huffed. "He *still* didn't choose me. I offered to be his mistress. I killed her off and hinted that I could be her replacement. And he didn't want me. Only for a quick fuck. An easy lay, like you've been doing with Renzo."

Giulia's foot reached back. She was right there, stepping through the billowing curtains. Her body remained inside, but she was nearly to the balcony. The second she was within my reach, I'd jump and knock her to the side. The element of surprise would be in my favor, and I had to pray that Dean was having luck reaching the room from inside the house. He was supposed to be breaking in to reach the door from the hallway, and I refused to give any thought or worry about why he hadn't shown up yet.

"No. Renzo and I—"

Isabella cackled. Her immediate laughter was sharp and hysterical. "Do not tell me that you love each other. Do not dare."

"I do. I do love him," Giulia admitted.

It was the first time she'd said it, and it wasn't even for my ears to hear, but she'd put it out there. I felt her affection when we made love. I saw the commitment in her eyes and I heard every ounce of desire and desperation for me when she spoke or cried out in ecstasy.

And I loved her too. I hadn't had a chance to tell her yet with all this going on. We'd clashed so quickly and our connection built so swiftly, we hadn't found a moment to have this sort of a conversation. As soon as I killed her mother and secured her elsewhere, we would. I would not let another day go by without her understanding that she and I were breaking the curse of our parents' issues.

"Love?" Isabella scoffed. "You're insane if you think he could care for you at all."

"He does." Giulia's voice rose with a little more confidence as she brought her other foot back toward the balcony, measuring her steps and likely trying to avoid looking like she was running or retreating too hastily.

"All the Bernardi men care about is themselves, fucking who they want and doing as they please. And that's why, Giulia. That's why this had to all happen now. I couldn't let that little whore carry my husband's baby. No other woman would ever bear Rocco a son—even after his death."

"Fine. If that's what you've decided was necessary, fine." Giulia cleared her throat. "But it has nothing to do with me."

"The hell it doesn't. If you keep fucking Renzo, you'll get knocked up with a Bernardi baby. If you're not already."

That sounded like heaven, the vision of Giulia's stomach swollen with my baby. It would be a dream come true to start a family with her, and I wouldn't stop practicing and making love to her until it happened. I wanted her—as my partner, as my wife, and as the mother of my children. I'd never felt more convinced that it was meant to be until hearing this vile woman swear to prevent it.

"And no Acardi woman will have the son in the wrong hands. You will not splinter the Acardi influence further by having a bastard with that man."

"Then I won't," Giulia shouted back. "All right? I won't. I'm packing up to leave with my sisters. We'll be gone and no longer your burden. You can do what you want with your power, and I'll leave you to it. I want nothing to do with this life anymore."

"Like I'd believe *that*! You just said you loved him, that he cared for you. The second you run out of here and try to leave this life, he'd just follow you and still get his way."

"No, I—"

"Only I will have the power, Giulia. Me. I will be the matriarch of the Acardis. Even if you fuck up the arrangement to marry Nickolas, this will all still be mine. Now that Dario's gone, I don't even have to deal with his interference, either."

"He's..." Giulia took another step back. If she moved out here just a little more, she'd be fully past the flowing curtains that gently floated around her from the breeze. "He's gone? *You* killed him?"

Isabella huffed. "No. But I led him on to think that you were captive at the Bernardi estate. The guards could take care of his breaking in to try to save you. Not like it's hard to shoot a slow, weak man like that."

"You bitch!" Giulia lost her control. She snapped, yelling like that.

Gunshots were fired as she lunged back into her room, and I knew that was my moment to move in.

Gripping the railing firmly, I launched myself up and over the barricade. I landed on the balcony roughly, but I didn't give myself a chance to gain my feet and stand fully. Jumping up and toward the women in the room, I aimed for Giulia.

She was down, hissing and grimacing in pain with her hand slapped over her upper arm. Blood slid over her skin, and at the sight of her wounded, I lost my temper. Any faint thread of control I had was severed.

With a guttural roar, I dove for her and knocked her back down to the ground, rolling so my body would be between hers and Isabella's.

Giulia's lunge at her mother had thrown her off balance. It'd knocked her onto her ass further in the room. Panting and grunting, the Acardi scrambled to rise to her knees, then onto her feet, sticking her gun back up in the air and aiming it at us.

"No! You will not do this!" She screamed it as her rigid face almost broke into a scowl. Even in her deepest rage, at her craziest moment, she looked too smooth and unaffected. She'd altered her face so much that she lacked the ability to truly show us an expression of loathing to match the growl in her words.

I breathed hard, staying positioned in front of Giulia as she leaned back, cowering behind me. She reached low to the carpet, making herself small as I braced for impact.

Isabella bared her teeth as she pointed the gun straight at my head. I stared at her, determined to let her see that I would never back down.

In this moment, everything else faded.

I was going to die. Right here, right now. This vindictive bitch lusted for my father and couldn't accept defeat. She'd murdered my mother and accidentally poisoned my brother. And worst of all, she'd dared to harm the woman I loved.

I saw nothing but the darkness of her evil stare. My skin went numb, and I gave up on the fury that I'd lost my gun in climbing up here. I heard nothing but the thunder of my pulse in my ears, waving back and forth as I waited for my last moment to come. Zoned out, with tunnel vision, I focused on letting her see the rage that I would always hold for her alone.

Fuck. You.

A dark hole appeared between her eyebrows. Her forehead remained unlined as her eyes went vacant, glossy as death struck.

I blinked, belatedly realizing that as I locked into the realization that I would die, a gun had been fired. But it wasn't hers. Her arms lowered and the gun tilted within her grip, aiming at the floor.

The low angle saved me. She pulled the trigger now, perhaps as a knee-jerk reflex, and I tensed at the searing slice of the bullet against my leg. The report of her gun prompted a follow-up.

Another shot rang out loudly.

Her torso flinched as another bullet sank into her chest, rocking her backward.

Again. Another shot.

The third hit pierced her heart and tipped her body to fling toward her left.

More sounds filtered through my mind past the ringing of the gunshots so near my head. I snapped out of the trance, hearing Giulia breathing hard right behind me. She panted, sucking in deep breaths before audibly swallowing. As I turned, broken from the reverie as Isabella's gun thudded to the carpet, I noticed the gun Giulia had pointed at her mother. She held it firmly, her arm raised so she could fire over my shoulder at the woman. Her fingers trembled, though, and as she stared, wide-eyed with shock that she'd killed her, her arm began to waver.

"Giulia."

I spun around, not needing to see Isabella fall to the floor. I felt the vibration of her impact, and as I twisted to haul Giulia into my arms, I finally exhaled the breath I held when I looked death in the face. Holding her shaking body reassured me. The panic receded. Peace would be a long time coming after the suspense of facing off with that psychotic woman, but with Giulia in my arms, alive and clinging to me fiercely, I knew that all would be right once more.

"Renzo, I..." She sniffled, worked up and near tears as she smashed her mouth to mine. Her kiss kickstarted me back to normalcy, to the overwhelming heat of love that consumed me from the inside out.

"I was so scared she'd—"

Now I silenced her frantic words. Kissing her again, I shifted to block her view from the dead woman on the floor.

"I've got you." I cupped her face and rested my brow against hers, staring into her eyes as our breaths mixed between our lips. "I've got you."

She nodded, leaning in to kiss me again. I tasted the salt of her tears, and I dove in to kiss her harder, needing every bit of this connection that we could lean on to reclaim stability after the storm.

"And I got you," she whispered.

The door smacked against the wall, and men rushed in. We both turned in unison, sucking in a breath at the sudden noise.

"Renzo?"

Dean staggered inside, his gun at the ready. His right side was bloody, but he stood.

"Giulia?" An Acardi guard entered beside Dean, and the man helped my guard stand steady as he wavered in his steps.

"Francis." Giulia lifted her hand. "We're here. It's done."

Before fully acknowledging what Giulia said, the Acardi man locked his focus on Isabella slumped lifeless on the floor. With a nod at her words and a deep sigh of relief, he lowered his gun. Then he nudged for Dean to lower his. "I *told* you she knew how to shoot."

Dean nodded, cringing in pain. "I see that now."

Witnessing my right-hand man and this Acardi guard not trying to kill each other should've amused me. As I stood with Giulia, careful with her wounded arm, I realized this would be the new norm.

The Acardi and Bernardi rivalry was over. The cause of it all was dead.

As soon as I saw to my bride's injuries, I would be celebrating that fact with her. All night long.

29

GIULIA

Giulia

"You're certain that they were out of the house when she came into my room?" I asked Francis.

He nodded, overseeing the doctor sewing up the stitches on my arm. It was just a grazing, fortunately. When my mother shot me, it wasn't with a decent aim. I'd lunged at her, so furious at her casual dismissal of Uncle Dario that I couldn't stand there and stall any longer. She'd missed me, only grazing my arm with her bullet. I was lucky. And I would never forget it.

The less I focused on the sting of the injury, the more I was prone to dwelling on the fact that I'd killed my mother. That wasn't all of it, though. I'd killed my father's murderer. And my uncle's. Sure, it was self-defense with her aiming her gun at me. Kill or be killed.

When Renzo showed from the balcony and gave me cover, I had just the right reach to grab my bag that had fallen off my bed when I was packing to get my gun.

The guilt—if any—would come later. Right now, I had to make sure all was well in the house I'd never call home again.

"Yes," Francis replied, furrowing his brow as he supervised the doctor tending to me. He stood over me, guarded as ever. "I left to follow Isabella, knowing Dario would find you and tell you to take your sisters. I had a bad feeling about leaving them here with the staff, and I came back. I got them into the car to go to your cousin's before I headed upstairs."

I exhaled another long breath of relief. If my sisters had overheard that fight... Or worse, if Marianna or one of the younger two had tried to burst in here and save me...

"Thank God they are safe."

He nodded, glancing up at the Acardi men dealing with the mess. My mother's body had already been taken out. I hardly cared what happened to the room. All the blood in the carpet could stay. I didn't give a damn. The whole house could burn down for all I cared, but then I felt bad about displacing the staff who depended on their jobs here.

Especially you. I offered Francis a weak smile. "And you, too."

He nodded gravely. "I'm sorry I wasn't here to back you up in time."

But I wasn't alone. Renzo had come after me, just like I'd hoped he would.

I'd saved him, but he'd gotten me to the position to do so. We'd ended up collaborating as a team. Partners. And the one person who'd set up the rivalry that kept us apart would never cause trouble again.

It's over. I stared at the spot where she'd dropped, knowing that remorse had no room in my mind. I was glad. I'd done well to end this, and I would come to terms with it one day.

"If you're ready to go...?" the Bernardi soldier said to me as he left the men he'd supervised in cleaning the room up. Both Bernardi and Acardi soldiers worked together in here.

"Almost," I told him.

He looked more like a capo, yet not. But I appreciated his due diligence to obey Renzo's orders to bring me to him once I was fixed up.

"Only once she's finished with those stitches," Francis argued.

Seeing these two men enter the room at the same time showed how quickly times were changing.

Before Renzo left to deal with his men outside and then with Giovanni at home, who he said had sent him here to kill Isabella, he introduced me to the older soldier. Dean. He was Renzo's newly appointed right-hand man, formerly assisting Luka. He'd come as Renzo's backup, but in fighting the Acardi guards most loyal to my mother's influence here, he'd been shot. Francis realized he wasn't the enemy, only trying to stop Isabella from killing anyone else. They'd teamed up to break in and help us, but I'd already done the deed.

Isabella Acardi would never hurt or kill anyone ever again.

Despite Francis and Dean in here, as well as the soldiers, I suffered a gnawing need to see Renzo again. Our reunion had been violent and brief. I hadn't kissed him long enough to reassure my heart that he was fine, that we could survive together. While I understood that he needed to hurry to his father and deal with breaking this news to him, I realized that I simply felt safer when he was near.

"Will someone see to his wound, too?" I asked Dean.

He nodded. Renzo had been injured too, with a bullet that flew awry as Isabella died from my shots. It couldn't have been a horrible wound, but I worried again about how he'd limped and compressed the spot on his thigh as he left.

It felt good to be in the trusted care he offered to back up the Acardi men here, but I wanted *him*. I needed to see him and truly convince myself that it would be all right to celebrate life again after so much death.

The moment the doctor nodded and gave me his approval that he was satisfied with his stitching, I stood and followed Dean out of the house. Francis promised to come later. If not to personally guard me at Renzo's place, then to head to my sisters and watch over them.

They didn't need to run away now. We'd find a new home and a new life here. In the meantime, with our mother's death, some distance would help. I'd go to break the news to them once I spoke with Renzo.

Talking didn't seem to be on his mind, though.

I arrived at the Bernardi residence that Renzo claimed for himself, and as soon as I entered the massive building, I knew that with time, my short stay in the dungeons at his father's estate home would be a faint memory. Staying in the past did no good to anyone, as evidenced by my mother's hatred for Giovanni. I had only the future to look forward to.

Renzo must have been watching for my arrival because he strode straight toward me. He was still on the phone, speaking with Giovanni by the sounds of it. Multitasking, he locked his heated gaze on me as he took my hand. A curt nod at Dean was all the acknowledgement he was going to give him.

With his smoldering stare sizzling my skin as he watched me walk with him, I smiled slowly.

He urged me to head upstairs with him, almost pulling me with his impatience.

"Weren't you wounded?" I asked, worried about his leg with his haste to get upstairs.

"Weren't you?" he shot back as he slid his phone to the side.

I grinned. We'd both fought tooth and nail to get to this moment, and

I would never forget it. Renzo wasn't my enemy. He never had been. How could he be when we fit together like partners so well?

On the way upstairs, he continued to streak his gaze over me, like taking inventory. His concern touched me, and I swore I fell that much more in love with him.

As soon as he led me into a massive, dimly lit master suite, he closed the door behind him. I curled into his side, kissing his cheek.

"Later," he said abruptly into his phone. He hadn't been listening, anyway. "Gio, I—" With a growl, he hung up.

"I bet you've got a lot to talk about with him," I said before he dove in for a quick, hard kiss.

"Later," he repeated as he picked me up. He cringed immediately and set me back down.

"You were injured, remember?" I said as I let him guide me toward the bed, pressing kisses over my face as I ran my hand along his jaw.

"So were you," he said. "Which means instead of dealing with these sleeves…" He tugged on the buttons of my blouse. They went flying, pinging on the floor.

"That was quick," I quipped as he unclasped the front of my bra next. We kissed between words and touches, removing our clothes as he backed me to the huge king-sized mattress.

"This will be…" he promised as he helped me lower his pants and boxers. "Fast." He grabbed my ass and pulled me flush to his chest. "Hard."

I smiled against his lips.

"This time, it will be fast and hard. I need you."

I stepped out of my skirt and panties as he led me back. "I need you now," I agreed.

Going from killing my mother to fucking my lover seemed like a jolting shift. It was a whiplash of emotions, but somehow, I craved his touch and that addicting bliss he could give me. After the horrors and threats we'd dealt with, we were due for the opposite.

Love. Security. Relief.

"But later," he said as we lowered to the bed together, our lips a breath apart, "I intend to take my time with you."

"Is that so?" I taunted, hugging him as he urged me to roll with him.

I lay under him, reveling in the strong weight of his body blanketing me. Every inch of his hard flesh warmed me, burning me up with raw desire that had me panting and desperate for him to fill me.

"Yes," he growled, leaning on his knees to wedge my legs apart. Again, when he put pressure on his wounded limb, he cringed.

I frowned, staring up at him. "I don't want you to be in pain."

"I *am*." He shifted us again, guiding me on top so I straddled him. "Right here," he clarified as he lined his erection up with my pussy. I was soaked already. Just kissing him got me so aroused and slick with juices to welcome him inside.

I grinned at his groan as I sank over his cockhead. Hearing this man admit that he longed for me and craved me to the point of pain was a heady thought to hold on to. With every thick, hard inch of him that I sucked inside my cunt, though, I lost the ability to think at all.

"Now, Giulia," he ordered. His fingers dug into my waist as he urged me to ride him. Although he was lying down and I was the one moving on him, he still instructed me. He still dominated. After too much time being controlled by men, I should've been annoyed. Instead, I relished his demands. They pushed me to please him.

I rocked on him, letting my clit get the friction against him with each grinding move. Impaled on his cock, I let him squeeze my ass and push me to ride him as he wanted.

Fast and hard, just like he'd warned.

My breasts swayed and jiggled, and the motion seemed so erotic that it brought me closer to coming. Too close.

He reached down to rub a circle around my clit, and that was all it took to destroy me. I clenched tightly on him, feeling the burst of my orgasm to every frayed nerve ending. Coming this hard, this quick, I felt fried alive. Shot into the air and sinking to float, all at once.

He jerked up into me once more, flooding me with his hot cum, and as we rode out the waves of pleasure together, he pulled me down until I rested on his chest.

"You are going to be my wife," he said as we caught our breath.

I smiled, my cheek pushing on his pec. "Am I?"

He continued lazily rubbing my back, and each pass of his fingertips on my skin teased me to break out in goosebumps.

"Yes." He leaned down to kiss the top of my head.

I lifted my face to crawl up and get a real kiss. "I love you, Renzo."

Nothing could keep us apart.

"I love you, too. And I'm going to make you my wife."

I grinned and cocked my head to the side. "Just like that?" I teased.

He nodded, smiling back with that roguish smirk. "Yeah. And that's final."

I can't wait.

Finally, I was where I belonged, with him.

30

RENZO

Renzo

T wo months later...

I glanced at all the paperwork Dean had dropped off to my desk. I loathed dealing with any kind of busywork like this. Secretaries could handle most of this shit, but these documents were a personal matter.

Securing Giulia's sisters' safety was a large undertaking, and I didn't want to slip up with a single mistake.

Marianna, Lucia, and Beatrice moved in with Giulia and me the week before our wedding. All the girls belonged here with us. Francis, too. I depended on the Acardis' guard to help with smoothing out a lot of the details about these sisters, but still, it was a lot to wade through.

With Giulia's marriage to me, her assets transferred to me. But her sisters' funds were a trickier dilemma to work through. Since Isabella had passed away, and Dario had too, there were some contesting relatives—mostly all distant—who slowed the process.

I'd be damned if any of them were screwed out of their Family's wealth. When leaders were killed, all kinds of people would swoop in to take what they could. But Giulia had me, and her sisters had us. Even though the Acardi name had raised them into a world of hatred, courtesy of their mother, they would have the full backing of the Bernardi name now.

Giulia Bernardi would see to their futures.

My wife. I grinned, excited every time I thought of her as mine now. She was, fully and completely, mine forever. And it was the reminder of her being my wife that helped me to deal with all this stuff.

When I wasn't here busy seeing to her sisters' futures and wealth after the breakup of their Family, I was taxed with dealing with the Romanos. Nickolas hadn't cared much that Giulia was taken. He'd been opposed to the marriage with her, partly because he thought marrying a Greek Mafia daughter would turn out better. Marcus was a hard sell on that business deal, but after word got out about Isabella's plans, he seemed happier to have avoided her.

Still, I was stuck dealing with business more than I wanted to. I delegated constantly, refusing to micromanage like Luka had. With Giovanni's new health issues, though, it seemed that I was damned to spend most of my time working instead of enjoying my new wife.

Now more than ever, I was feeling the full, oppressive weight of being the eldest son. Giovanni wasn't dying anytime soon, but his slowing down like this was a reminder that one day, I'd be at the head of the Family.

With Giulia as my wife, though, I knew I was fortunate. She was my partner, quick-minded and sharp to give her input on businesses. She would never be some woman to dismiss as the mother of my kids.

"If we ever have time to start on that," I grumbled to myself. With our adjustment to merging the Acardi and Bernardi names with marriage, I wondered if we were too busy to try to start a family. I didn't want to delay. We had the rest of our lives, and we made love constantly, even if they were stolen moments of passion.

"What was that?" Giulia asked as she entered my office. She set *more* papers on the desk and perched on the edge of it.

"What happened to everything being electronic?" I complained of the documents she'd brought in. They looked like more addendums of her parents' wills to review.

"Paranoid Mafia Families back everything up on paper."

I sighed, angling her to fall into my lap instead of sitting on my desk.

"What were you grumbling about?" she asked again.

"Being too busy to do what I want with you."

She kissed me, tender and sweet. "And what is that?" She was acclimating well to this life with me, and she was no slacker in keeping busy and helping with what she could. Yet, our passion had yet to fizzle out.

"Getting you pregnant." I kissed her harder, loving the sexy mewl she gave me. "Starting a family."

She pulled back and smiled wide. "I wanted to wait until next week on your birthday to tell you…"

My heart raced at her playful smile. "What?" I laid my hand on her stomach, and she covered it with hers. The diamonds on the ring I gave her glittered like sunrays.

"Surprise," she said before kissing me again.

"*Surprise?*" I mocked. "With how often I need you?"

She giggled lightly, peppering me with kisses as we stared into each other's eyes.

"And I will always need you," I reminded her with a deeper kiss.

Her announcement filled me with joy, so much that it felt hard to draw a full breath. "I can't wait for our new future to begin."

No longer bound by an old rivalry, we were heading into a bright beginning.

One of our choosing.

Printed in Great Britain
by Amazon